THE TERMINARCH PLOT

PLOT

The Five Rims Series: Book 1

by Roger Colby

This is a work of fiction. Names, characters, places and incidents either are products of the author's imagination or are used fictitiously. Any resemblance to actual events or locales or persons, living or dead, is entirely coincidental.

The opinions in this manuscript are solely the opinions of the author and do not represent the opinions or thoughts of the publisher. The author has represented and warranted full ownership, and or legal right to publish all the material in this book.

For my Dad, who loved a good adventure story as much as the next guy.

Special thanks to my Beta Readers:
Lorraine Kruskopp
Rita Colby
Carl Williams

Cover Art:
Chris Wren

A very special thanks to my awesome science consultant:

Mr. Michael Dean

Chapter 1

Guillermo's patience shriveled away as he waited on
the drug cartel rep, draining his third cup of j'umaa,
completely unaware that in the next few days he would
become the sole member of his race. He stared at the
empty plasteel cup, the bitter black liquid drops all that
remained of the j'umaa, and then scanned the crowd for
any indication that any one of the bugs recognized him.
His dark hair was soaked with sweat, and he kept an old
tattered scarf tied like a noose around his throat even in
the steamy humid daylight. The bipedal bugs walked
past his table nearly oblivious to him, and he thought that
to them he might look like any other Terran.

They, consequently, didn't care.

They didn't seem to get emotional about anything
really, since Terrans figured out long ago that bugs don't
seem to have the capacity to feel, at least not in the way
Terrans understand emotion. He was sure the bugs had a
name for themselves as a race as well, but their "speech"
was a complex series of body language and pheromonal
emissions. The Terrans simply called them "bugs". The
bugs didn't seem to mind.

He stared at the few drops of j'umaa left in his cup,
wondering if ancient bugs read the grounds in the bottom
for fortunetelling, and he thought about Meagan.

Meagan and her addiction that took her from him,
ruining any hope of parenthood, her life ending in a pool
of her own blood.

His badge and gun long gone, that part of his life over now for a year, he thought that perhaps he could have saved her, could have done something different to insure her survival. That part of his past had been pushed to the back of his mind, replaced with desperation and the need to live a life of acceptable means, of good food not tainted by the organics that permeated everything on this planet, of a place to live where he didn't have to constantly keep one eye open. He was weary of the job into which he had been forced.

He'd found another gun. A bigger one, but not too big to hide under his long coat, and this one was modified thanks to Gunny.

The bugs scurried by the railing that circled the little outdoor cafe, all of them of different colors representing their castes, the light from the street lamps reflecting off of their large black compound eyes. He was thankful that the dingy white tables were vacant in this mid-morning hour, except of course for a couple of bug waiters who were counting through their tips. He tried not to go out in public as he was sometimes recognized not by ordinary citizens, but by the ever vigilant security forces who found him last time. He'd dug the identichip out of his back with a razor months ago, placed there the last time he had been detained. He wasn't about to get picked up by some noob cop on a mission. Couldn't afford that.

Those few Terrans who knew him figured Guillermo didn't have anything to lose, what with his race becoming so few. The rebels, long before Guillermo was born, decided to lottery out the Terran living arrangements

3

after the rebellion was over and the Phaedran Empire went belly-up. Some (mostly the criminal element in this city) felt that Guillermo's actions since his initial crime had been the heroic beginnings of a new rebellion, this time one led by the Terrans, and some saw it as a sad gasp of air from a drowning race.

Actually, most everyone thought the latter.

He'd often confessed to Gunny over drinks that he wished his great-great-grand dad would have been with the masses that the rebels sent out into space, those hedonistic Terrans of the Phaedran Empire. The Terrans had finally lost the war of attrition, forced to file on board those ailing world-ships the Terran ancestors had used to limp to the Five Rims after fleeing their own solar system. More than likely they were all dead now, leaving this little Terran enclave the only remnant of their race to survive.

It was pretty pathetic, really.

Guillermo's violent exit from the security force had been the subject of weeks of news stories on the feeds, then a manhunt, then a brief mention between commercial breaks and then in passing when some lucky investigator would track down a lead. The only Terran to ever serve the security force gone mad and on the run for assault and various other crimes.

On a nearby screen mounted over the door to the restaurant, the eerily quiet bug commercials sold more mindless products, their strange hieroglyphs scrolling along the bottom of the screen.

They had all but given up the search for him, some thinking he was dead.

The subject of interview shows that needed ratings bumps would sometimes raise the question as to why he had betrayed his fellow officers. Guillermo had watched from the safety of the Undercity the countless interviews and talking heads who guessed that Guillermo had become sick of being the only Terran cop in existence, or that when his wife died he lost it. Perhaps he felt like their whipping boy, someone to punish for the sins of his ancestors. He washed out of academy the first time only to barely make it the second. Many felt that he was the Terran poster child for why his species couldn't be trusted. Maybe he got tired of holding the line. Got tired of being their stooge. One day he snapped, attacked his commanding officer over the treatment of some Terrans who stole food, nearly killed a few of his squad. Shot his own partner through the abdomen.

It was food. Just food.

McFly, his partner, had lived and was assigned his case.

To spite being a fugitive, Guillermo was currently calm and collected. As usual he was broke again. The money from his last job had been eaten away or shot away or gambled away, and he was sitting in this little cafe waiting on a meeting with some bug middle-man, and probably he would soon go to work for someone else who would treat him like a dog. He hated being out in the open, exposed like this, but the instructions stated…

"You Guillermo?" said a clicking, vibrating voice, shaking him out of his current thought. It was a brown skinned bug who suddenly sat across from him at the table, and now he stared at the expressionless ovoid black compound eyes and the five sets of mandibles that clicked together and vibrated to mimic Terran speech.

Bugs learned Terran via a leftover device that originally served a dual purpose. As designed, a bug would stand before the device and place their nimble hands in a black box mounted on the front of it which would then lock on to them so that they could not remove their hands until the session was over. Two holographic faces, one bug and one Terran would mimic words in silence and if the machine's unfortunate pupil did not mimic Terran speech correctly based only on sight the mimic box would send a white-hot overload to the bug's pain center.

Mimic boxes were since modified to omit the little black box, replacing it with a red and green light.

Guillermo sat quietly, his eyes staring through the brown skinned bug.

"You...Guillermo..." asked the bug again.

"Who's asking?" Guillermo growled, enunciating so that the bug could read his lips. Guillermo could smell the faint aroma of a pheromonal cue, the method by which bugs talked to each other normally. Guillermo didn't possess a sensitive enough nose to read it, though, but he'd become adept at discerning their body language.

This guy was nervous.

The visitor reached forward with a clawed, exoskeletal hand causing Guillermo to brush his fingers across the butt of his modified pulse rifle just under the table. He hoped that the guy he bought it from, unlike the last guy he did business with, didn't sell him a dud. The bug's hand pulled back as quick as it had thrust forward, and then this un-named visitor stood and walked into the crowd of shuffling insectoids. There on the dingy white table in front of Guillermo was a small slip of antiquated paper, brown and dirty. He reached for it and turned it over in his grimy fingers to find a set of three numbers written there, coordinates for yet another meeting place.

He was getting the run-around.

"Guess I'll call you 'Mr. Goose Chase!'" Guillermo shouted after the bug messenger.

Since bug names were unknown, impossible to be heard, or even utterable by Terran speech, Guillermo, like most Terrans, had taken to giving names to bugs based on how he felt about them. Currently Mr. Goose Chase was just that.

After stuffing the paper inside his coat pocket he dropped his last two chids on the table with a metallic clink and then walked across the street to straddle his bike, a rusted, oily beast of a machine. With a brush of one thumb over a metal stud, the old hover bike roared to life, making the sound of two asteroids mating. Her sleek design was marred with dings and scratches and a few heavy welds where some hasty patching had been done after the Terran guns had been removed from it ages ago. Her blocky nose, a metallic, battered horses head with one cyclops eye of an intake turbine, hissed and whined. She shot out waves of blue lightening from her lower emitters, scattering loose gravel from the road as she

lifted Guillermo March shakily off of her retracting
landing skis.

"Built to last," he muttered, and kicked the thrusters
in gear.

Ugly blue lightening shot out from under her as he
pushed her out into the foot traffic. Wary bugs skittered
away from him, not out of fear but out of self
preservation. He hit a couple of switches to pump more
juice to the grav-levs and he began to ascend above the
swarming crowd, a few of them ducking when the fusion
rods adjusted and sent out a loud pop that echoed off of
the storefronts and upper level windows of the more
affluent of the lower crust of bug society.

He swerved, purposefully striking a limping traffic
drone when it got too close. He glanced absently behind
him to see it satisfactorily spiral downward out of control,
sparks flying from its round exo-casing. He then pushed
the throttle up to eighty percent and merged out into the
hover-lane to blend into traffic that swarmed like c'zez
after a rain storm.

As he flew along, he punched in the coordinates he
had seen on the paper and his nav-computer led him
straight to the top of one of the ancient slightly curving
chitin spires that ringed the outside of the city. He hoped
he would be meeting the Death Adder this time instead of
one of his lackeys, because he was ready to go from small
time to the big time.

His talents were being wasted with petty thievery.
Drugs were where the real money was, and he was
hunting a big fish. It was about time he was paid his

worth. All of that training, all of that groveling on the bottom rung. He wanted vindication.

He could see the landing strip ahead, a prodigious oval metallic platform that was built into the side of the ancient chitin structure far above the upper hover lanes, its anchors biting into the chitin surface of the tower like a sliver of steel embedded in flesh. Several bug toughs stood quietly on the platform, all of them brandishing illegal weapons, their faces incapable of expressing emotion as understood by Terrans, and no Terran had ever witnessed a bug emotion. He landed his bike in the middle of the platform with a blast of electrical arcing and was immediately surrounded, the guard's weapons emitting the signature high pitch whine of plasma cells powering up.

He dismounted, his eyes coldly staring at the hired muscle, his bike powering down automatically since he was no longer seated on the saddle. It would remain that way forever until it sensed his facial identitat.

"Death Adder," he said, making sure the guards could see and hopefully read his lips. They didn't, and two of them, whom he had given the names "Muscle One" and "Muscle Two" began to hiss at him and he could smell the faint aroma of fresh flowers. This was one of the scents he recognized.

He was being insulted.

He opened his tattered grey coat and it flapped in the high wind that whistled around the platform. This exposed a modified pulse rifle hanging by his side, and they moved in, unhooking the magna-clip that held the rifle in place. He allowed them to take it, but his eyes told another tale. One hand undid the scarf from his neck and he gritted his teeth.

He had his eyes locked on the rifle as there was a hiss at the end of the platform and a door opened near the tower, a shaft of red light silhouetting a shadow. Mr. Goose Chase appeared, his head cocked to the side, his empty arms outstretched in a common greeting. The mandibles clicked and whirred.

"Welcome, officer March," he said, his Terran mimicry monotone and without inflection, an eerie side effect of the old machine that taught them to speak.

"Just March," mouthed Guillermo, no need to make vocal what could not be heard. "Glad that someone speaks Terran. You going to take me to Death Adder or are we on another dinner date?"

"No weapons," said Mr. Goose Chase. "Come quickly. He is not to wait."

"Yeah," March said, his voice a whisper. "Your goons already made sure of that."

Guillermo's face did not betray the fact that there were two more palm sized pistols they missed.

He entered the red-lit tower and prepared to climb the treacherous spiraling tunnel that led up to wherever it was that Mr. Goose Chase was leading him. His Terran fingers had trouble gripping the odd hand-holds of the corkscrew tunnel, but Mr. Goose Chase had little difficulty. Guillermo managed to hang on, but by the time he reached the middle of the journey his forearms were on fire. He managed not to slip, and Mr. Goose Chase did not wait, only looking back at him periodically to click his mandibles together in what Guillermo had come to recognize as what passed for bug amusement.

Guillermo understood this test. He could not work for this organization if he was not prepared to meet them on their terms, climb their crazy spiraling tunnels that had been carved into this spire when Terrans were just figuring out how to efficiently kill one another with nuclear bombs.

As he reached the top, he found a room carved out of dark brown chitin lit with luma-rods and archaic candles. It smelled like a bug den, which is to say odorless. Not antiseptic, not foul, but ominously odorless so as to allow the bugs to communicate in silence using their pheromonal cues. This also told Guillermo that not much had been spoken here, at least anything he could detect with his inferior olfactory nerves.

But he had recently had a cold.

As he gained his footing in the room, he saw that at the end of this spherical chamber stood two of the largest Guajiin he had ever seen, every bit of three meters tall. They had all four of their thick arms folded over their broad chests, their enormous tusked lower jaws jutting out, their blue facial tattooing covering half of their pale, pacyderm-skinned, bald faces. Their beady dark eyes fell on him like a wash of black water. Sitting between them, his five sets of mandibles clicking together, was a weak looking little bug, his arms and legs wrapped in shiny gold material that glittered in the reddish light of the room.

Bugs didn't wear clothing on their abdomens. They needed to breathe.

"Officer March," clicked the little bug. "We finally meet. I am called Death Adder."

Guillermo fought a laugh.

"It's about time," Guillermo said, keeping his hands dangling at his sides, remembering his social signals. "I can't say it's been a party dodging the law while waiting for us to have this meeting, but it hasn't. As a point of fact I really didn't appreciate the run-around."

One of the Guajiin, the one on the left, snorted and curled his heavy lip. Guillermo tried not to flinch.

"I'm hungry, tired and need a shower," Guillermo continued without a beat. "And by the way it's just Guillermo."

One of the massive Guajiin, the one who curled his lip, put one lower hand on the butt of his oversized pistol, the device his race used to settle all disputes.

All disputes.

With a wave of the bug's small, claw-like hand, the thick arms folded again, and it was only now that Guillermo noticed that Mr. Goose Chase had vanished. Guillermo's lips pursed as he briefly wondered where the guy went, but he had to stay focused, and the small bead of sweat running down his left temple was trying to damage that purpose. Guillermo hoped that Death Adder couldn't recognize the meaning of his body language.

Guillermo's eyes squinted and his mouth twitched.

"Relax, Guillermo," said Death Adder, his mandibles taking extra care to pronounce the Terran name but failing with a slight vibrating lisp. "I had to have time to make sure that you were indeed free of your friends at the security force. Someone of my station does not make a habit of making mistakes."

"No worries," said Guillermo, keeping his eyes trained on the Guajiin, yet wondering where his original escort might have gone. "It's been a little over a year, after all. I'm not in the news anymore. You don't have anything to worry about with me, sir. I'm pretty sure my last altercation with the cops would be proof enough."

"Yes," chittered Death Adder, his large black eyes eerily reflective. "Your last...unfortunate business...was a poorly calculated exercise. How can I insure that if you were to work for me that you would not make the same... miscalculations."

Guillermo glanced at the chronometer on his wrist and one of the Guajiin flinched. The Terran raised an eyebrow and absently marveled at how quick such a large creature could move. He wondered if he could get to his hidden pistol in time if things came to that.

"I've made mistakes, yes," Guillermo said. "But I really need this job, and it's the only thing I've got going that'll ensure I have plenty to eat, and none of that unprocessed stuff that is killing us off. Besides. I figure you need me to reach the Terran junkies. Somebody who doesn't click when they talk."

Guillermo glanced at his chrono again, thinking about Meagan...how she died. This would all be over soon.

"Is there some place you need to be, officer March?"

"It's Guillermo. And no, I don't have any place to be.

Let's just get on with it, shall we?"

There was a pause, and the two Guajiin stepped away from the little chair where Death Adder sat quietly. The bug produced a small writing pad made from a scrap of brown ratty paper. Guillermo was motioned forward by a flick of a clawed hand, and as he approached, he saw that Death Adder was writing a string of numbers using an archaic graphite pencil, something the Terran hadn't seen at all in his thirty years of life. He wondered absently where the little bug had managed to get one of those, and then he understood why no one was able to trace Death Adder's communiques to his network of drug dealers. He wasn't using traditional digital means. Probably used a system of couriers who left little slips of precious paper all over the city.

It would look like so much trash to the untrained eye.

Guillermo could feel the ominous presence of the Guajiin guards and their heavy gaze (and their stink). He stepped slowly forward, standing uncomfortably close to Death Adder who was writing what Guillermo knew were equations, chemical equations that when followed produced Volos, the drug that had become a cancer to the Terrans, just another nail in their coffin.

The nail that killed Meagan.

As Guillermo rubbed his thumb and forefinger in a strange back and forth motion, he knew that the low frequency signal produced by the now activated homing implant would alert one of little Death Adder's lackeys. Somewhere within this massive spire they monitored that kind of thing and he would have to move rapidly.

"I need a new chemist," said Death Adder. "My old chemist was…found to be in the company of someone… unsavory. You will find another chemist for me. Money is no object. You will have a ship, and I will send you to any of the five rim worlds to find them. Deal?"

"Certainly," Guillermo said, then repeated the word for Death Adder when the drug lord turned to read the Terran's lips.

The little bug hissed and then emitted a foul rotten odor that made Guillermo's eyes water, and he read that as satisfaction. Guillermo turned to the doorway he had entered earlier to see good old Mr. Goose Chase appear, shuffling swiftly toward them, his three toed feet pattering on the chitin floor.

"Detain," said Death Adder crumpling the slip of paper and then turning to face Guillermo. Before he could move, Guillermo suddenly felt four giant hands grab him from behind, holding each of his limbs in an iron grip. He had heard about the Guajiin drawing and quartering Terrans during the rebellion, but now he thought he might actually experience it first hand. He tried not to let it melt his resolve.

Where was that infiltration team he was promised?

Guillermo felt his joints grind as he was hoisted from the floor by one of the Guajiin guards. The four-armed thug, he surmised, probably felt joy at being able to finally kill one of his ancestor's hated enemies, an enemy who probably had made his four-armed great grandfather work in a mine until he died of dysentery or some other horrible disease. Guajiin were all about the racial debt, and Guillermo cursed his predecessors for enslaving generally every race in the Five Rims.

"Hold him still," clicked Death Adder. "My colleague informs me that you have a tracer beacon embedded in your flesh…officer…March. Gront will now throw you from the landing platform."

Guillermo's mind spun, the adrenaline coursing through his heart, clouding his thoughts, and then he spoke.

"I really don't know what you are talking about. And for what it's worth, that's probably not a good idea, *v'oshtu.*"

He could feel the massive leathery hands tighten up on his extremities, the Guajiin profanity probably the trigger. Guillermo's hands and feet were immediately pricked with tiny invisible needles that spread to his fingers and toes.

"It is not profitable to lie to me, officer March," said Death Adder, living up to his name. "I am never witness to any violence perpetrated by my staff. Besides, I just had my office cleaned. Gront, please take this spy outside and deal with him. I have to readjust my living arrangements because of this fool."

Gront didn't say a word, but carried Guillermo toward the door, the giant's heavy boots clomping thickly on the chitinous floor.

"Wait!" screamed Guillermo. "I can explain! They made me do it. They told me that if I did this they would let me off. Give me a fresh start. Please understand."

But Death Adder and his assistant were already

gathering his notebooks and stuffing them into a small satchel.

"Juice another Terran," growled Gront, his voice a resonant bass that vibrated Guillermo's torso. "Why not you snuff it high lofty instead sad shame road?"

The Guajiin never mastered Terran sentence structure, as its syntax was difficult for the way their brains were wired. Guillermo understood the giant, and decided to answer with more profanity.

"Because I'm Terran, v'oshtu," grunted Guillermo defiantly. "How about we settle this with a duel?"

Gront did not flinch at this, his loyalty to Death Adder more important than his own cultural laws, but slid down the tunnel with his charge, only to stop abruptly at the landing platform. Guillermo could hear the wind whistle across the opening. The four arms still gripped him tightly as Gront marched across the platform toward the edge, effortlessly carrying Guillermo like a medium sized doll, his huge boots clomping along. Muscle One through Four were standing around Guillermo's hover bike, their guns holstered, and one of them was touching the leather saddle with one nimble clawed hand.

Soon all Guillermo could see was the Royal City skyline, the ancient chitin spires circling it like the outer cilia of a venus fly trap, thousands of blinking hovercars and flying vehicles darting around the maze of skyscrapers within. The humid wind began to pick up, and his hair whipped around his face, the sweat cooling his skin.

Time to act.

Guillermo tightened his bottom lip, curled his tongue and whistled a predetermined tone causing his hover bike to erupted into a concussive ball of flame at the command. It consumed the surrounding guards, the shockwave knocking Gront to his thick knees with a crunch. The big tough had let go of one leg and that was all Guillermo needed. He clicked his boots together, produced a small blade that popped from his heel, and then he promptly used this to kick backward and stab Gront in the abdomen.

Gront roared in pain and then dropped him, only to reach for his gigantic revolver at his hip. Guillermo was already on him, dropping to the ground and somersaulting backward to spring up into a focused body leveraged punch to the sternum that amazingly caused Gront to reel. The fuel from the bike, a flaming puddle of oozing gelatin containing the charred corpses of the hired muscle, popped off a glob of burning pain onto Gront's exposed skin. As Guillermo centered his fighting stance, his fists at the ready to take on a being twice his size, the Guajiin speedily drew his pistol and fired. The massive bullet, certain explosive death with a dead-on shot, instead shredded the flesh of Guillermo's left shoulder, severing his arm, and leaving a mess of blood and tissue that forced a scream from his lips.

He sank to his knees on the landing platform, his hand grasping a gaping wound that gushed a spray of hot red blood.

Gront stood to his full height, rubbing his abdomen

with one hand and reaching to pull the hammer back on his rune-engraved pistol, when he was washed in the blue light of a security force interceptor that hovered just off the platform. Suddenly the tarmac was filled with rappelling bug tactical soldiers, their green skin shining where their matte black protective suits didn't cover them. The bug security task force had finally arrived.

This didn't stop sneering Gront from getting revenge.

He barreled forward, but before he could fire his gun the hand holding it was blown from his wrist by a blast from a nearby interceptor, a white-hot bolt of plasma that caused the giant's gun and his attached hand to thump to the platform. Gront screamed a deafening roar before diving toward Guillermo only to be caught in the electro-net that had been deployed to capture him.

Guillermo rocked backward on his knees, then stood slowly to his feet near the edge, his hand holding the gushing wound in his shoulder, and he watched the tactical soldiers move into the spire, their guns at the ready, the black knight of unconsciousness trying to overtake him.

The wind.

The wind caught him, moving him like a slip of dry paper.

As he fell backward, his ankles crossing, he stumbled off into the void, falling toward the street hundreds of meters below. He absently thought that it had been a dangerous year of working undercover in the shadowy underworld. As he fell, head toward the ground, he looked out over the upside-down haze of Royal City and he was glad that his death had mattered, that he had finally avenged Meagan. A smile spread across his lips with the understanding that he had helped cut out a cancer from the flesh of the Terran race, that maybe they would survive a little longer without the horrid drug Volos.

As the humid wind rushed by him, he breathed in a strangely calm breath, blacking out before he ever reached the ground.

CHAPTER 2

A steady static squeezed through his stuffy ear canals. Something sickening and sinister like a serpent slithering down a hole. Guillermo tried to move but found that his arms and legs did not respond and he could feel that some kind of bond had been strapped across his chest which kept him frozen in place. He tried to open his mouth and smacked his parched lips, his tongue clicking on his palate like a castanet in a sandstorm. His eyes opened to darkness and he wondered for a brief moment if hell was real.

And then he saw something move, something quick and shining.

He began to hear alarms, not the kind he was used to hearing in the street and on the job that he had shirked to go deep undercover, but the type that accompanied the tragedy of emergency rooms and the busy nature of trauma wards. He tried to speak, but could only manage a grunt, and then something wet and cold was being squirted into his eyes, washing away whatever had caked them together. He felt the pain of it on his eyelids, the crusty flaking gunk that accompanied a long sleep.

"Guillermo?" said a series of clicks and guttural vibrations mimicking the pronunciation of his name. "Can you hear me, partner? It is so good to see you awake after so long. We have to catch up, as you used to say."

He could smell something, a pheromonal cue that he vaguely remembered a bug expressing when he had accidentally spilled the beans about a birthday or…what was it? He couldn't remember. His mind was swimming in the sluggish soup of second-hand senses, as if he was experiencing all of this through one of those old fashioned VR helmets.

He tried to speak again and only managed to cough, his throat a paper tube filled with sand. His vision washed in and out, and then came the nausea. And then he was off into the void again.

Falling.

Falling.

Falling.

He dreamed there.

A massive chitinous spire rose out of the ground before him, and he stood on a plain of sand that stretched to the zenith from east to west, north to south. A wind wafted the strands of his black hair, flapping like tiny flags in his eyes, and he brushed them aside to see the spire rise higher, chunks of rock bursting forth from the ground that formed bizarre words that he couldn't read. The spire jutted upwards where it grew like a massive thorn before a pale sky. He could feel the ground shake as the shockwaves from it slammed into him, knocking him to the hard sandy ground, knocking the wind out of him.

"Again!" he heard someone scream, and looked around to see no one near him.

The spire continued to grow, and suddenly he was being drawn toward it on the wind, a crumpled leaf of a man, his arms and legs helpless to stop him, straining, reaching toward the ground only to float away toward the spire, and now it was not a spire but a mountain, a massive spike of rock that jutted far into the sky, far above the atmosphere of this strangely familiar place. He screamed, or at least he tried to, but he did not make a sound. His lungs were on fire, and he noticed now that he was suspended in space above a massive planet, the mountain rising from one side of it making it oblong in shape, and there was a massive hurricane on the front side, a desert on the leeward side.

"Again!"

He was punched in the sternum by a force unrecognized, and now he sucked in cool air, his lungs thanking him for the pleasure of breathing.

When he managed to open his eyes he saw the large black ovoid eyes and clicking mandibles of his old partner McFly, the partner he had been forced to shoot through the abdomen a little over a year ago. Had to make sure the underworld knew and believed that he had indeed turned from his job as officer of the peace, the only Terran on the force.

He had secretly enjoyed it.

There were several others in the room. He rolled his eyes around, trying to get a grasp of where he was, what had happened. He remembered the fall, and then he looked down at his left arm to find a set of metallic rods held together with shiny metal bands. They were jointed in the middle and near the end where a delicate, five fingered bronze hand lay motionless beneath what he could only surmise to be a shimmering blue stasis field.

He looked away, trying to steel his resolve but not being very successful, and all he could manage was a soft grunt and a squeezing together of his eyelids to allow a solitary tear to roll down his cheek. His lips pressed together tightly, and the second grunt that emerged from his throat caused him to suck in a breath. He coughed on thick saliva that quickly built up in his mouth. He opened his eyes again only to see a couple of bug medical staff rushing in to administer what he assumed were sedatives, helping him drift off to sleep. He fought it as long as he could but drifted away a prisoner of the drug.

In the haze that was sleep he did not dream, but when he woke again, his body aching, he saw that he was alone in an antiseptic room, shiny metal walls all around. Various instruments and machines sat beeping and whirring, and the soft glow of a ceiling that was one solid light source cast a weird green hue upon the room. He was surrounded by blurry, glowing geometric shapes.

The shadows cast by the instruments made strange
designs on the floor. To his left, a circular onyx door was
recessed into the wall.

He looked down, hoping that his arm was indeed a
dream, only to realize the horror that was the truth. It
had been replaced with a cheaper alternative to a
genetically grown graft, commonly used for amputees.
He stared at the shiny silver rods strapped together with
bronze colored bands, the elbow joint a smooth ball, his
hand a bronzed articulating set of five fingers and an
opposable thumb. He tried to move it, but it only
twitched in the static energy of the stasis field. He could
lift his head, but the rest of him was strapped down by
the invisible dome.

He called out, managing a weak whine like that of a
small child who had awakened from a nightmare. His
legs, covered in a soft yellow blanket, would not move
either, and he desperately wanted to scratch an itch that
had begun to tickle his nose.

"Hey!" he croaked, his voice raspy. "Could somebody
help me sit up at least? Great *Volɓuun*, I just want a
drink."

In a few moments the circular door irised open and
three bugs skittered in, their mottled red skin and huge
compound eyes reflecting the soft glow of the ceiling
illumination. One of them clicked out a command and
the light suddenly became brighter. This caused
Guillermo to squint, unable to move his hand over his
eyes to shield his vision. He could faintly smell the
pheromonal communication of the bugs as they began to

orbit his bed, their little exoskeletal hands waving through holographic images and adjusting instruments. After a few clicks and chitters he could move his right arm and he immediately rubbed his nose, thinking absently that there were so many simple pleasures that one took for granted, namely scratching an itch. He was hampered a bit by the tubing stuck in the bend of his arm which caused him to crane his wrist around because he couldn't fully articulate his elbow.

"What the crulls happened to me," he pleaded, staring at his robotic arm, trying to touch it and feeling the static charge of the stasis field. He was still unable to move it. "Can anybody speak Terran?"

They continued, not ignoring him but not speaking his language, one of them turning to look at him and only managing what looked like a shrug. He took the opportunity of the bug's gaze to re-state what he just said, but he was only met with another half-executed shrug.

"That's great," he muttered. "I'm stuck in a hospital with a bunch of gimps who can't understand me."

They continued working, one of them now holding a small device that beeped and whistled, not that it mattered to the bug who did not have the ears to hear these annoying sounds. Guillermo reminded himself that these machines were left-over tech from when his race dominated the Five Rims, and he was pretty sure those annoying sounds meant something important, medically speaking.

Relief came in the form of a green-skinned bug who walked slowly into the room through the irising door, the

familiar gate of investigating officer McFly, his partner
for two years.

"You are looking more fit," McFly said, his mandibles
clicking together to form Terran words. "I am so pleased
that you did not expire."

"Yeah, yeah. Save it," Guillermo shot back. "I really
need a drink. None of that unprocessed swill, though.
I've earned it. Bring me some crulling eighty proof."

McFly folded his hands in front of him, his mandibles
clicking together as if to say something but then didn't.
He then turned and grabbed a small stool. Sitting atop it,
Guillermo's partner placed one clawed hand on the railing
of the bed and tilted his head to the side.

Guillermo immediately recognized this body language
as the bad news dance.

"I will have the health attendant service your needs,"
said McFly silently emitting a pheromone which sent two
of the other bugs out of the room. Once the door irised
shut and they were alone with only one other health
attendant, his partner leaned slightly forward, folding his
hands in his lap.

"I do not want to alarm you, but you were near death
when we rescued you. We managed to snare-net you
from mid-air, but not before you had struck a passing
traffic drone. You sustained much damage, and you have
only now awakened from a three week slumber."

"Yeah, so," grunted Guillermo. "Did you guys get
Death Adder and his goons? Are they going to harm any
more Terrans?"

McFly continued as if Guillermo had said nothing.

"Our medical team is limited in that not many of our doctors are trained to treat Terrans. You remained clinically dead after they stabilized the damage from the Guajiin weapon. Some of the shrapnel from the shell was lodged in your lung and in your left ventricle. It was difficult to remove, not because we did not have the tools, but because you were so close to death. They had to revive you numerous times."

"So why not a grafted arm? Nobody wants to spring for a decent arm? What the crulls, man?"

"As I have told you on numerous occasions —"

"Yeah, yeah. The crullin' profanity. Go on."

McFly shook his head side to side in a momentary blur, what amounted to bug frustration and then continued.

"Certain developments have occurred since you were successful in bringing Death Adder to justice —"

"So you jailed the little twerp. Good. I think losing my arm is a small thing compared to that v'oshtu loose in the Five Rims, right?"

"Yes," said McFly, lowering his head. "It is a great sacrifice you have made for your people…and Meagan has been vindicated…but."

McFly sat in silence, and the machines around them blinked and whirred, the I.V. pumping another round of fluid into the Terran's body. Guillermo absently wondered if it had been filtered of the slow organic poison that permeated every drop of water on this planet. Surely it had. This was a hospital, after all.

"What's eating you?" asked Guillermo, his

understanding of bug cues somewhat limited, but accurate enough to know that McFly was avoiding a real let-down.

"A bomb went off in the Terran enclave two days after you were brought here," he said, his mandibles clicking methodically. Guillermo's face became ashen, his jaw falling open.

"As far as we know," McFly said flatly. "You are the last of your kind."

CHAPTER 3

When Guillermo slept, if he slept, he dreamed of the crimson spray of his blood floating on the high-altitude winds near the spire, or he dreamed of Meagan's soft skin only to wake and find none of these things. Only the stark, cold walls of the hospital room.

He lay in the dark most nights with his eyes wide open, yet not able to shake the images of the past year, the hunt for the cartel who had distributed a drug that had become a deadly worm eating away at the heart of the Terran enclave, taking his wife. Someone had been slipping the highly addictive Volos into purified water and Terrans had been ensnared in its deadly euphoria. His mind endlessly played the secret plans they had made to bring down Death Adder and his underground network. He had been forced to shirk all that he knew and loved, live a lie, and now that he could finally grieve his wife, he found himself instead to be utterly numb.

Nothing could cure Terrans from Volos addiction and the withdrawals were deadly. He had to find out about her death through second-hand channels six months prior when he was suddenly public enemy number one, after his own plan that he had spent weeks organizing was in full swing. He had been left wondering if she was coherent enough to be disappointed in him.

He didn't even get a chance to mourn her, couldn't mourn her.

She was at least spared the moment of blinding heat of the bomb that extinguished the Terrans from the bug planet, from the Five Rims, from probably the entire universe as far as he knew.

And the v'oshtus wouldn't let him leave.

He had spent days in complete silence, staring out the window of his room at the aerial traffic, sometimes weeping, sometimes punching the plasteel window, sometimes screaming.

When he couldn't sleep, and this was often, he called for the orderly to bring him more pain-killers, but soon that was deemed unnecessary as his arm had "fully accepted the cybernetic implants" and his brain "had begun to accept the new appendage".

He wondered if he could vote about the usefulness of his arm.

He still couldn't control it properly. The arm often moved in his sleep due to the firing of some random synapse. This always woke him, the arm some independently controlled monster attached to his body by internal anchors and a supply of neuromimetic substances coursing through his veins. These substances produced by nanites, allowed the machine to effectively work in tandem with his brain's electrical impulses.

So far it had been like learning a new sport.

Or riding a unicycle.

On a tightrope.

Daily he was roused from his insomnia by an orderly he'd named Bedpan, a silent bug who did not understand or speak Terran, who forced him to rise, shower, and dress. Bedpan would then coax him first with rewards and then threats to follow him to a cold room down the hall from Guillermo's meager quarters.

He felt like a favored pet.

In a cold room he would often endure yet another humiliating foray into what the bugs called physical therapy. Guillermo felt it was more of a form of old Phaedran Empire torture coupled with a seminar in shame and humiliation. Bedpan would leave him in the room alone for a time, which to Guillermo felt like an eternity. At first he had shuffled to the round door in an attempt to leave, only to find that Bedpan had locked him in. In one corner of this antiseptic white room floated an onyx black monitor orb which allowed the bug doctors to watch him in case he tried to harm himself as he had done on at least two occasions.

Most days he would sit and stare at his brass hand, flexing his fingers and balling up a fist, tears filling his eyes. Sometimes he would test the tensile strength of the mechanical tendons by pushing against a wall, listening to the metal pop and then mend itself via the nanites releasing the neuromimetic chemicals.

The thought of small robots coursing through his veins sometimes gave him nightmares.

After weeks of asking to leave in order to pay his respects to the dead, Guillermo sat alone in this antiseptic, white room, his watery eyes fixed on the brass fingers of his new mechanical hand, mesmerized by the way it looked through his tear-filled eyes. He had managed to will it to rotate around so that he could see the palm, the metal there covered in a thin layer of course yet pliable plastic. The fingertips were coated with this substance as well. His doctor, a shorter than normal bug, had told him that he would need time to learn to use the limb, that he would have full functionality within a few weeks, but the brain needed time to learn to fire the proper nerve clusters.

He wished he could rip it from his torso.

He sighed deeply, his wish to leave the hospital to inspect the damage to the Terran enclave denied yet again and he ached to discover the string of clues that could possibly lead him to the perpetrators. McFly had been placed in charge of the investigation by the Queen herself, his expertise in forensic reconstruction unmatched anywhere on the bug planet. Guillermo, however, understood a different brand of investigation, the kind that involved finding any leads, using his fists to pound the life out of them until they gave up a shred of a clue, and then following those threads until he reached an inevitable conclusion.

The security force knew that Guillermo would bring his own brand of justice, a justice reserved for the schoolyard or the back alley. They only responded with a repetitive message, like a skipping music file, some story about how he needed to recover first, to learn to use his new hand-me-down arm. In good faith, McFly had been by to talk him down on numerous occasions, once literally when Guillermo escaped and stood on the roof ready to jump.

McFly had convinced him not to try base-jumping sans parachute.

Guillermo would sit most days and stare out the window of his room, the vehicles flying by inaudibly, the transition shade built into the plasteel adjusting as the bright daylight became the orange hues of sunset. The Terran spent most of his time staring at his metal arm, flexing the rubber-coated fingers and then making a fist. The bugs and the Hegemony they belonged to did not spend any time researching the Terran cloning tech that was so prevalent during the reign of the Phaedran Empire, choosing to focus more on hover vehicles, plasma weapons, star-drive, mainly the day-to-day tech that kept the Hegemony of the Five Rim worlds connected and operating. Terran replacement limbs were sort of low on the list or not on said list at all.

Guillermo was constantly assured that the Hegemony, the sole monopolizing entity for Terran tech, was "working on it."

He had decided to not lose sleep over it, but so far sleep had evaded him. Since the coma, when he managed

to sleep from sheer exhaustion he only managed to enter a
nightmare world of night terrors. Every time he managed
to shut his eyes his mind overloaded with images of the
Guajiin bullet severing his arm, the initial shock of
watching his mangled appendage float away from him as
if in zero gravity, the oddly peaceful state of falling upside
down toward the ground, and then a recurring dream of
his body colliding with a mountain of Terran skulls. He
tried not to think about it, tried to shut it out, but he kept
reliving it again and again with the medical team
monitoring him day and night via holo-feed.

Psychologists had been brought in eventually, but all
of the sessions so far had been unproductive, and he
refused their drugs.

He had christened the psychologists with some pretty
obscene names.

Again in the rehab room he turned toward the little
black orb floating in the corner and glowered at it, a
single tear rolling uncontrollably down his cheek again.
He had been assured that searches were underway for
any possible Terran survivors, and they were scouring the
planet diligently to find any of his race that had been
absent at the massacre. It had been two weeks now and
the search parties had not been successful. They told him
again and again that they would not rest until they found
them.

Assurances.

He wrapped his fingers around the metallic wrist of
his mechanical arm and pulled, then grabbed it closer to
the shoulder joint and pulled yet again, but it had tendrils

that anchored it deep into bone and he felt a twinge of pain behind his left clavicle. With difficulty he pulled off his white linen shirt, the short sleeve hanging for a moment on his metallic wrist, nearly ripping the fabric. The new arm did not respond as he wished and he had to grunt and tear the shirt to remove it from his arm's metal edges.

He stared at the seam of flesh that met the metal plate anchoring the arm to his frame, how the various shiny metal rods erupted from his pectoral muscle like fibrous tendons of steel. He ran his finger down the edge of the seam, the pink scar tissue a jagged reminder of his loss, and then he rapped on it with his knuckles, his teeth gritting in anger.

The arm was not programmed for tactile sensation at the moment, and he was assured that this would happen with time.

Just as he felt a scream building in his throat, the oval door irised open and three bugs scurried into the room.

"Officer March," said his taskmaster of a physical therapist. "You have removed your shirt. That is excellent work."

"Yeah," Guillermo growled, using his right hand to wipe at his eyes, his mechanical arm dangling. "I just wanted to see it. Now I just want to pull it off."

"That would be fatal, Guillermo," chittered Seymour Butts as the other two bugs took vital signs with small hand-held instruments. One of them plugged a small device into a port at his mechanical wrist. "Perhaps you should try putting the shirt back on?"

"I was hot…and I ripped it a little," said Guillermo, gently pushing away an instrument that came too close to his face. "I like not having a shirt on. I'm such a sexy beast since the surgery."

The bugs stopped for a brief second, but went right back to flicking their fingers through holograms and hovering about his examination table.

"I apologize," clicked Seymour bowing his large blue head. "I sometimes forget that Terrans use humor to mask pain."

"I'm not masking anything," Guillermo said as the other two bugs left the room. "I just don't want to put the shirt back on. Can I have the freedom to do this? I am the last of my kind, you know."

"It would be a good exercise to get used to the new arm," said Seymour, ignoring that last statement. "I insist that you try."

Guillermo turned to face Seymour, speaking slowly so that his lips could be read plainly.

"I insist that you take a leap from a spire."

The bug shook his head side to side in a blur.

"I have no intention of ending my life. Terran emotion is something of a hinderance to your recovery, it seems, but is only a minor setback. Perhaps you should try to mask your…feelings for a time. Your use of the arm will be much more fluid if you —"

"If I what? Blocked out the pain of losing everyone I know? Are you crulling kidding me? When are you bugs going to get that I don't give a whiptail's offal whether I recover or learn to use this freak arm you gave me? I just want to get out of this hospital, arm or no arm, and start figuring out what happened. Start finding the scum who set off the bomb."

Seymour shook his head again.

"I assure you, this is being handled. Your partner McFly is scheduled to meet with you in a few days to update you on the progress they are making. He is...we are all...concerned that you will not recover mentally."

Guillermo sank back on the arm he was born with, snorted through the back of his throat, and spat a chunk of mucus in the bugs face.

Seymour staggered backward. His type-pad clattering to the floor as he began to click and chitter, the air around Guillermo filling with a sweet smell of pheromonal insult as the bug did his best to wipe the spittle from just above his mandibles.

A grin cracked the gloom of Guillermo's face, something that hadn't happened in weeks.

"I am glad I can be of amusement to you, Guillermo," Seymour managed to click together in a stammering, unorganized manner, now reaching for a nearby towel to wipe at his face. "But if you will not work with me then you will only lengthen your stay with us. It is unfortunate that you would behave in such a manner, but then I expected such barbarity from a Terran."

Guillermo sat up and slapped the back of his neck with his hand, leaving his mouth open, producing a hollow popping sound.

"Yeah," he chuckled. "I got more of it right here for you, bug. I guess the best of the species was spared."

This was too much for the bug, who shuffled out the door and left it open for Guillermo to go back to his room, but Guillermo sat on the exam table, slumping forward, his laughter winding down until they converted to sobs as he covered his mouth with his mechanical palm, his tears running down the cold chrome back of his hand.

He pushed his arm away as if it belonged to someone else. As far as he was concerned it did.

CHAPTER 4

Sleep seemed to be something of a fantasy for Guillermo for the next few days. He lay in his new hospital room, accommodations upgraded to something like a hotel. He often stood at the window staring out at the city, the countless hover-vehicles zipping by like a swarm of bees.

He had tired of the holo-vid projector and its constant news about the bombing. The bug protests were growing by the day, demanding a more speedy process to finding the perpetrators. Reports were sketchy as to the events leading up to what was now being called a terrorist action. The talking heads, their words spelled out below them in bug hieroglyphs, speculated on conspiracies and political second guessing. The Queen had intimated her belief that the public needed to trust in the security force to determine the guilty party or parties. The Council of Eight blamed the Terrans themselves, saying that it was a terror attempt gone wrong, stirring the rumor mill with unsubstantiated reports of Terrans who were plotting to detonate a bomb outside the Council headquarters which "mysteriously backfired." Guillermo did not believe the Council, as their draconian policies in the days leading up to the bombing soured him to anything they might say. Their insistence on forcing the Terrans to live in one concentrated enclave, their laws that resulted in Terrans becoming second-class citizens, and their general racism toward his kind left a sickness in Guillermo's stomach that wouldn't go away.

All was truly lost.

So far no search party had located any Terrans anywhere on the bug planet, and Guillermo began to stare at the palpable loneliness of being the last of his kind. It pressed down on him, a weight of unfathomable magnitude.

Toward the third evening after moving from a constant care room to a minimal care ward, he was again pushing his utensil around in a plate of unrecognizable protein and native vegetables, all of it processed heavily to remove any contaminants. His eyes were drawn to the silver hypo lying on the table next to his bed. It had been issued by his therapist, good old Seymour, a pacifier to help him sleep. He had now decided that he was going to inject himself with it. He was tired of fighting and just wanted rest.

The thought crossed his mind that perhaps he could request a larger dose, something to help him join his fellow Terrans.

Wiping a few tears that had collected in his eyes with his thumb and index finger, he reached for the hypo, his eyebrows rising slightly at the feeling of the cool metal registering on the rubberized fingertips of his mechanical hand. Apparently the nanites were doing their job, knitting nerve cells together. He stared at the hypo for a few seconds, then shrugged and pressed the nozzle to the side of his neck.

He thumbed the activation stud.

He heard the signature hiss of the hypo as it injected him with the sleep agent and he set the cylinder down again and then lay back against the pillow, letting the drug take effect. His eyes gently closed as he listened to the steady thrum of his barely perceptible pulse.

At last he did begin to sleep, the waves of cool murkiness flooding over him gently, but then he felt an unusual twinge of pain and he thought that maybe he had rolled over on his metal arm again. When he opened his eyes, however, he saw the blurry image of three figures surrounding his bed.

One of them had a small plasma pistol, the kind gamblers hid in their sleeves.

He fought sleep, trying to keep his eyes open as he yawned, and he could hear the clicking of mandibles forming Terran speech.

"Thought you could fool us, didn't you Terran," said a hissing voice. "Did you think you could hide your survival from us? Death Adder sends his regards from prison."

Death Adder, Guillermo thought. *Hadn't they executed*

him by now?

"There is no need to call out to your attendants, Terran," came the husky clicking rasp.

Guillermo opened his eyes enough to see the two bugs on either side of his bed grabbing his arms and then strapping a cord across his chest, forcing him down onto the bed. He saw the third, the one speaking, activate the stun setting on the plasma pistol, and Guillermo knew that at point blank range it could kill. It would be a slow death, the electromagnetic surge overloading various parts of the brain, concentrating on the pain centers mostly.

"You boys best get this over with," Guillermo managed, his speech slurring. "And you better kill me, because I'll grease all three of you if I get free."

The bugs all stared at one another for a moment and then continued with their task.

Darkness began to seep into Guillermo's vision as the drug took hold of his brain again, but he fought through it, and the bugs methodically moved to the side of his bed and pressed the end of the barrel to Guillermo's forehead. He managed to kick his legs out, causing the bed to jostle, allowing him to free his mechanical arm. The arm flung wide, smashing into the table near him with a loud bang that popped the wrist and caused the hand to tear free and bounce across the polished floor. In the haze, Guillermo stared at a jagged line of metal and fibers that protruded from his wrist.

The bugs emitted an odor that faintly registered in Guillermo's nostrils as he managed to use his jagged wrist to stab at one of them. The Terran rolled off the bed, fell to the floor and banged his forehead against the corner of the nightstand as he dropped.

The dark flooded in on him, but he rolled under the bed only to be dragged violently across the floor by hard grasping fingers. He felt a stab of white pain in his side as he was kicked in the ribs. This woke him enough to force his eyes open. He saw the plasma pistol being switched over, the signature whine of the emitters warming up to produce a deadly gout of white-hot plasma.

"We were going to make you suffer, but we will have to deviate from the orders a bit. I'm sure Death Adder will forgive us."

"That v'oshtu still alive?" Guillermo croaked. "You fail his orders, he'll kill you, too."

Guillermo tried to stand then, noticing that at least one of the bugs lay on the floor near the bed, a stream of yellow fluid gushing from his face where the sharp edge of Guillermo's severed wrist had sliced him open.

He absently named him Squishy.

"Glaaggzzzttt!" clicked the gun wielding assailant nearby, pointing his weapon at Guillermo over the bed. But Officer March stood shakily, his mechanical arm raising in defense as he rushed forward and struck at the gun, the white-hot blast burning a black line in the ceiling as the two of them struggled, the hospital bed squeaking and groaning as it was knocked aside. The second bug backed away as Guillermo managed to clumsily grab the gun, climb up onto the bed and then push off, using his

superior weight to drag his assailant to the floor. The gun
slammed to the hard duracrete and the hair trigger caused
the gun to fire off a round, blasting a jagged hole in the
window, nearly missing the other bug who was now
barreling toward the two of them.

Guillermo felt himself begin to slip away again. He
drew in a deep breath and screamed as he jammed the
jagged mechanical stump into the vulnerable thorax of the
bug gunman again and again, just as the other bug
grabbed a handful of his hair and pulled so hard that
Guillermo thought his scalp would be pulled from his
skull with the force of it.

A string of profanity shot out of Guillermo's drooling
mouth as he rolled to his left and his bare foot kicked out
in rage at the backward knee joint of the bug. He
listened to the crunch of tendons as the door to his room
irised open and he saw a blurry figure who looked like
Bedpan. The light from the hallway outside was a hazy
halo in his vision as he heard a snap of metal and a
crackle of electricity.

"Get some help!" Guillermo screamed, struggling to
right himself but scraping his metallic stump on the floor
and banging his head again. The hobbled bug who had
fallen nearby produced a small blade, crawled forward,
and began to stab Guillermo in the thigh. As the pain and
the drug began to finally win the battle for his life, he fell
backward into a sea of black oil, his lower extremities
feeling warm and unnatural.

CHAPTER 5

The next day as Guillermo sat at a cybernetic workstation, watching his new hand being attached to his broken robotic arm, he couldn't help but think about one of the many pre-colony holo-vids he liked so much, an epic story where a young fighter had learned some terrible news about his father and was getting a very unrealistic robo-hand installed. It felt good at least to be wearing normal clothes again and not a hospital tunic. McFly had brought him a gift of some Aldrassan made wuutrak hide pants and a spider-wool white shirt, something that had to be tailor made to his body type, and he thanked his partner profusely even if Guillermo felt like a real "dandy" for wearing such fine threads.

Guillermo managed a weak smile at his technician.

"You think you could put some kind of pop-out plasma gun in the forearm or something? You know. Get the drop on the next guy who wants get past your excellent security with a crulling plasma pistol."

"No, Officer March," droned the bug technician, his mandibles clicking furiously. "It is not possible to install such a device. The energy source alone would overload your nervous system."

"Kidding," said Guillermo, poking a finger into the housing that contained the delicate manipulator rods, only to be gently pushed away by the technician. "Yeah, yeah. I get it. This leg wound hurts like a v'oshtu."

McFly clicked his mandibles nervously.

"Your attitude must improve if you intend to be released, Guillermo," he said, his cold hand resting on March's shoulder. "The doctors want to make sure that your arm is functioning normally before they do so, however."

"And I guess the fact that someone wanted to off me right here in the hospital doesn't raise any alarms? If there are any Terrans left on this planet or anywhere else, we'd better make sure that they are protected, McFly. Somebody's finally going to make us extinct."

The two bugs looked at each other, their pheromonal cues faintly evident to Guillermo's senses. The quiet was unbearable for him, so he slapped McFly's hand away.

"You find anyone? You guys still on that? Or are you doing the same bang-up job you did keeping Death Adder's goons out of my crulling room? And how did he find out I was here, anyway?"

Silence.

He assumed the bugs were communicating somehow, or just nervous about talking to him about it, maybe trying to figure out how to say that he was indeed alone. McFly waggled his head from side to side, a sign of irritation. Guillermo decided to speak before he heard another excuse.

"If it wasn't for that attendant coming by I'd be a lump of ashes drifting on the wind right now," Guillermo growled. "Am I really safe here, anyway?"

"The Queen's bodyguard arrived just in time," McFly offered, his blank face incapable of expression. "She is securing your new room as we speak and is eager to meet you."

"I'll thank her personally. Have you been able to gain any headway in the bombing case?"

"I will need to brief you on the details, Guillermo, and I will need your help. The individuals who tried to kill you last night were not in Death Adder's employ. Death Adder was executed three days before you awoke."

Guillermo jumped as the techie jolted his mechanical fingertip with a small chrome rod, but Guillermo shot McFly a wide eyed glare.

McFly continued.

"As a matter of fact they had not committed any crimes before entering the hospital, one of them a gardener just north of the city. How they managed to procure a military issue plasma pistol is still a mystery. You see, since the bombing there have been some unprecedented assassination attempts on royal officials. One of them, a trusted attendant of the Queen's daughter for many years, managed to kill three chamber guards with a common stylus before entering the Queen's meditation room. He came within two meters of her majesty before being gunned down by our forces."

"Chert," Guillermo whispered.

"In fact, as I mentioned, I will soon need your help. There are forces at work here… But that is for another time. You need to regain your strength. We shall discuss these matters later. Perhaps over a bottle of aavriil."

Guillermo hadn't heard this term in a while. He remained stoic, knowing that aavriil was code for McFly wanting to say something to him in private, and that he didn't even trust the techie working on Guillermo's arm. Guillermo didn't let on, frowning, then growling out a response which let McFly know that he was on board.

"Well, I guess a bottle of aavriil will have to do."

"Guillermo," said McFly finally. "I want you to come with me. I know you have been avoiding it, but you need to see the damage first hand."

The technician closed up the forearm port with a magnetic click, foregoing the normal monotony of what Guillermo called the "pre-flight flap check" as Guillermo followed McFly out of the room, down the hall, then past a few doctors who at first made motions to stop them but dutifully stood aside.

Each doorway irised open as they walked through and eventually they emerged on a balcony overlooking the bustling city. The humid and mist laden wind, immediately comforting, felt like a refreshing shower after a long day of working in filth. The balcony stretched around the corner of the pyramid-shaped building, and they continued to walk, Guillermo following his partner's unusual side-to-side gait. When Guillermo rounded the corner he stopped, his eyes transfixed on the jagged lines of the ugly horizon.

He gripped the plasteel railing of the balcony, his metallic hand squeaking the rubberized fingertips. He felt his knees weakening, but he held fast to the railing, clearing his throat and trying to wrap his mind around what he saw. Two kilometers away, he judged, began a swath of unevenly damaged buildings and skyscrapers that looked as if a large meteor had fallen, leaving a massive crater of destruction.

His old apartment had been somewhere in the middle of it.

Vast support beams jutted out of the rubble like the broken and mummified fingers of a long dead giant, the cables and support rigging like metallic webbing, frayed and splintered. Work crews hovered in construction vehicles that hoisted huge chunks of debris away as thousands of others, all of them wearing yellow environmental suits, milled about the ground, plasma cutters sparking, an organized crew of termites chewing away at what the bomb had created. They had cleared most of it, leaving a dirty crater that left a deep curve in the foundation of the city.

Guillermo at first stammered, then hung his head, closing his tear-filled eyes to the horror before him, realizing that this was not just the Terran enclave he was seeing, but what remained of all of the outlying bug industrial district. As he had seen on the holo-vid in his room, the bomb had detonated deep within the enclave, but the resulting blast consumed the chemical factories nearby, erupting into a fire that had consumed nearly a quarter of the city before they were able to control it.

Many of McFly's people died as well.

"Your attacker had not committed any prior crimes," said McFly, staring at the ruin, then looking around to insure that they were alone before he continued. "As far as we know he was absolutely ordinary. He had been working near the hospital for three years, two months as a j'umaa vendor. No military training, no proclivity to violence, in a word a law abiding citizen of Royal City."

McFly handed Guillermo a small clear plastic capsule and inside was a pill shaped metal object about the size of a fingernail. It rattled around in the capsule, its metal surface etched with a string of Terran numbers.

"He had this little thing lodged just under his carapace right behind his left eye. As far as we can surmise this device is based on an older Terran design. The number etched on it does not fit with any pattern that we can find on record, and we have run it through every algorithm that the techs here on our planet can think of. It seems to act like a homing device, but it fooled every security sensor at the hospital, and also passed the deeper sweeps that the security force ran on every being that entered or exited the building."

"Why is it so important?" asked Guillermo, his voice low, trying to keep his emotions in check as his glassy eyes scanned the wreckage. "It's just a homing device. Big deal."

"No," said McFly. "I said it *acts* like a homing device. It was somehow controlling the j'umaa vendor, using him as a puppet. It is tech that is far beyond even the tech of the former Terran empire, possibly a heavy modification. I had it examined by an Under City contact, and he theorized that it produces a signal that causes our race to be highly susceptible to suggestion, that it was receiving signals as well as sending them out. All of that in such a tiny device. It is beyond nanotech, working on a higher level, altering the victim's brainwaves which are unique only to them. At least that is what we *think* it does. I am going to have my contact run some more tests on it."

"So who is behind this?"

"I feel like I am being watched at every turn, my friend. I have never felt more uneasy. Some of my conclusions are leading to levels of authority, the Council, something dark and unknown, and I'm not sure even the Council knows what is going on. I am not entirely sure I can make public what I am suspecting. In time the evidence will be revealed, and then I will perhaps be out of a job...or dead."

"Then who do you think it is? Are you saying that the Council is behind the bombing?"

After a long pause, McFly's mouth clicked softly, a difficult task for a bug, used when he wanted to be precise.

"Guillermo. I have come to realize that there may be a deeper conspiracy here than I originally surmised. I cannot say what conclusion I will reach, but I must be thorough, and that may involve some espionage on my part. That's where I will need you. Your underground contacts. The ones you formed while in exile."

"When do I start?" asked Guillermo, his voice a whisper.

"At this moment there is nothing for you to do, my friend," McFly replied, staring intently at his partner. "Until you have recovered from your injuries you have been placed on medical leave. But perhaps I can, as you say, pull some strings. I have to get you moving on this."

Guillermo set his face, his lips tight, his eyes narrowing.

"I'm never better, I guess," he growled. "It should be me down there figuring out what happened...who did this...I swear I'll make whatever v'oshtu responsible wish the Phaedran Empire was back. I might be the last one, but I'm going to make them pay."

"Guillermo, there are proper paths we must tread. There are some who are even suspicious of *my* involvement, and the protests are only now growing in strength. My people are horrified by this bombing, the death of the Terran race, and as of today I thought we had kept your survival a secret, for your safety. The attempt on your life was well planned. If not for the nanites you would be dead right now. They managed to cauterize the knife wound or you would have bled out in moments. Your survival has alarmed someone, but I need to have time to get to the center of this conspiracy, to ensure that you are safe, that all of us are safe."

Guillermo reached out with his mechanical hand and pressed one rubberized finger against McFly's chest.

"Nobody is going to tell me what I can and can't investigate. I made a lot of connections to the rotten underbelly of your world when I was undercover, and since they know I'm not vaped it doesn't really matter if I help or not. Right?"

"You have a point, my friend. Perhaps your new bodyguard can help us."

"Bodyguard. Who's to say she won't be a traitor. You scan her for the implant?"

"Yes, of course, had to use an ordinary magnetic resonance scanner, something used for diagnostics on fusion cores" said McFly, his hand resting on Guillermo's shoulder. "I think I may have offended her with the request, however. She submitted willingly."

"Better safe than sorry."

Soon they were no longer alone as some of the hospital staff began to stroll the balcony, part of their morning routine. Several of the bug medical staff were stopping to stare at the only Terran left on their planet. Guillermo began to nod his head, his mouth forming a wry smile that was barely visible as he scanned the damaged horizon.

"So you guys haven't a clue, then. Ok. That's fair. Just like a bug. Figuring out the mathematical equation that is going to get you from point A to point Q and then there will be the proper forms, of course. I don't care who knows I'm alive, but they better know this: I'm coming for them."

"I do not follow," McFly said, his head wagging back and forth, a cue that signaled confusion, but the bug had caught on to Guillermo's ruse.

"I should be helping you with this case," Guillermo said. "I'm the most qualified, and besides, it's my people that got flushed."

These words froze in Guillermo's throat, his eyes beginning to water again. He wouldn't cry right now, not in front of these strangers. He wouldn't show any emotion, be a bug. When he could do so without suspicion, out of view of any spies, he'd cut down to the bones of what held this crime together and then he mused on the idea of roasting the perpetrators alive, his primal

Terran instincts boiling within him.

"Many of my people were lost as well, Guillermo. Let us handle this."

Guillermo paused, making a show of holding in his anger.

"If you say you are on the case, then I'll trust that. We worked together too long for me to doubt your abilities as an investigator."

"Thank you for understanding," said McFly. "I sympathize with your loss, but cannot understand the pain of it."

A long and uncomfortable pause hung in the air like a thick cloud as they stood facing one another until Guillermo again turned his gaze upon the scarred city skyline.

"So what now?" Guillermo asked finally.

McFly waited until the crowd thinned and they were several meters away from any prying eyes.

"I believe some important evidence is about to surface any day now, and I will get back to you soon about the details. Until then I ask that you rest and let me handle this. I covet your faith in me."

"Done, pal," Guillermo managed a grin. "Sure thing."

They began the short walk back to Guillermo's hospital room. Once inside the hospital, as they shuffled down the crowded hallway toward the room they were met by a wiry bug, her mottled red skin signifying the military caste. As they approached, the bug stood at attention, her arms at her sides, and she addressed the pair in mimicked Terran.

"By the command of the Queen, keeper of the sacred nest, restorer of our people," she chittered. "I am tasked with your safety Guillermo March."

Guillermo's face reddened as he let out a burst of air followed by a bellow of maniacal laughter. The bugs nearby who saw it stopped and stared blankly at him. Guillermo stifled his laughter when he saw Seymour emerge from a doorway and pull out his tablet to jot down some notes.

"Forgive me, Officer March," clicked the bodyguard. "Did I say something amusing?"

Guillermo smiled.

"Oh, no. It's just a Terran tradition to bust a noob's chops. Are you who I have to thank for not being completely extinct?"

The bug stood rigid, her features unreadable.

"Really," Guillermo grinned. "I'd like to thank you for saving me last night, but I can take it from here. You honestly don't need to hang around anymore. I'm actually pretty boring anyway."

"Forgive me, Guillermo," said McFly. "The Queen has sent one of her personal bodyguards. This is a high honor. It would be an insult not to accept."

Guillermo looked at McFly for a three count and then understood that his old partner was giving him an unspoken cue. He decided to play along, and then fearlessly pressed a rubberized finger into the armored thorax-plate of the bodyguard.

"I'll call you Noob," he said.

"Noob it is," the bodyguard clicked. "Chamber guard,

second class."

"Good to meet you, Noob. What are your orders, exactly."

"I am ordered to guard you, sir, to ensure your safety even at the cost of my own life" said Noob. "I am sworn to your service."

There was a brief yet uncomfortable pause.

"If I may," said McFly. "The Queen only desires to assure your safety and Noob is her solution for now. Please allow…Noob…to do her duty."

"Great," said Guillermo, hands on his hips. "I suppose I'll go back to my room and visit the latrine. You coming?"

The bugs paused, staring at one another for a moment.

"I am bound to your service Officer March," said Noob as if reading directions. "I will accompany you, but first allow me to present this message from her majesty. It was what I intended to do upon arriving at your domicile yesterday evening."

She produced a small black orb that left her hand and floated between them, and all of the nearby bug hospital staff stopped to stare as a green beam of light was emitted from the orb, forming the image of a sleek Aldrassan female. Her large, lidless ovoid eyes, small mouth and elongated cranium the only physical difference that separated her from Terran physiology.

That, and she was bald.

"Greetings, Guillermo," she said informally. "I trust the bodyguard is satisfactory. Please accept her as a gift to you from her majesty. The Twelfth Queen of Set Six is troubled by last evening's unfortunate accident, and wishes to speak with you personally about this and other matters tomorrow."

"I'm busy getting a sponge bath from Noob tomorrow. Perhaps we can postpone —"

"Unbeknownst to you, your safety is important to the security of this planetary government and possibly the Hegemony we share as well. Please, Officer March. I will arrive tomorrow morning atop the hospital where we will move you to the palace indefinitely. Her majesty wishes to have audience with you there where she will explain the gravity of the current political climate and our dire circumstance. Your residence has been prepared at the palace. Until then, blessings on you."

She folded her six-fingered hands in front of her and the image flickered out with a visible flash of static and then the orb returned to Noob's hand.

"An honor indeed," said McFly. "You have been given sanctuary at the palace. We do need to have that drink soon, however. That bottle of aavriil is at the ripe age for consumption."

Guillermo looked at McFly, his eyes narrowing. McFly still needed to speak to him about something secret, something that perhaps even the Queen could not know. He would bide his time, do what he was told, and when the time was right he would speak to his partner and find out what he wanted to tell him…just not here.

"Sure, partner," said Guillermo. "Come on, Noob. Let me show you how play a Terran game. We call it five card stud. Hope you brought your chids."

Noob's shoulders slumped.

"Yes sir, Officer March."

CHAPTER 6

Guillermo stood reluctantly near his new companion Noob on the landing platform atop the triangular roof of the hospital, the Terran's heavy boot absently tapping at one of the many blinking landing lights. Guillermo, ignoring the bug, stared at the rubberized palm of his new hand, flexing the metallic fingers and then making a fist, the motion repeating over and over again. He felt like his real arm was underneath all of that metal, the phantom pain subsiding, and even though some of the feeling had begun to register along the thumb and just inside the heel of the palm, he still wished they would have been successful with the genetic graft. The surgeon had explained in a voice that sounded automated that one in a million recipients could not receive genetic grafts, and he had won the lucky lotto on that. He was thereby stuck with this cold metal thing that woke him several times a night like a rough steel rod in his bed. He was also stuck with Noob, but at least she was terrible at five card stud.

McFly, although invited, was not able to join them today on their jaunt to see the royal arm of the bug's constitutional monarchy, saying something about having to sift through some new evidence he had been waiting on, that they would share that drink later, and Guillermo thought that perhaps there was much that his former partner hadn't been clear about.

Namely everything.

He absently wondered if he'd have to share a drink with Noob as well.

His new bug companion stood stoically to his left, her constant protests about standing on the roof in the open becoming a grain of sand in the gears of Guillermo's mood.

"Sir," Noob said. "I insist that we stand inside the exit door, just until the Queen's envoy arrives. It is foolish to assume that you are safe anywhere in the open. As has been proven time and again, no one can be trusted."

Guillermo only smiled at her, letting out a breath of air that sounded like the hiss of a cornered animal.

"Would you calm the chert down? I get that you have a job to do, but I'm not going to cower in a corner. You just stand there looking like you're doing your job and I'll beg the Queen to reassign you when and if I see her."

Noob's silence bespoke her feelings on the matter, and Guillermo didn't have to decypher any of her pheromonal cues.

The skyline, seen through a haze of humid fog that had settled in the ruins, was outlined by the rising sun, sending fingers of light across the wreckage of the enclave and its surrounding residential buildings, many of them still lying in a pile of dust and plasti-crete mixed with giant chitinous shards pointing in various angles. The blurred lights of the early morning crews were just beginning their jobs, clearing away the debris now that all of the bodies had been found and recovered. The bugs had cremated them all, namely due to the sheer number of dead. They had ignored the Terran tradition of floating the deceased out an airlock, something that was a hold-over from the long journey here, but the Terrans were not present to exact their customs. The Council of Eight flanked by the Queen and her entourage had held a bug "death to life" ceremony instead, placing a small portion of each person's ashes on the tall spires that ringed the city and letting them float away as dances were danced in their honor.

Something about bugs dancing at the funeral of the Terran race made Guillermo sick.

His thoughts were interrupted by the tinny whine of a repulser engine and a blast of hot air as a hovering transport vehicle emerged from the mist above like some frightening bird of prey, the blast from its revving turbines blowing his wild dark hair around his head. Noob stood as if made of stone, her upturned face unmoved by the swirling air. Guillermo raised his mechanical hand to shield his eyes from the running lamps on the front of the vehicle as they briefly focused on the two figures before rotating down and creating blinding white spots of light on the landing pad. The engines gave one final scream as the landing gear extended and gently lowered the vehicle to the black plasti-crete, its wings rotating forward and up to reveal a door on the side. Guillermo tried to show that he had mastered the folding of his arms with little success.

He quietly cursed his prosthetic.

The onyx-black vehicle's side door slid open and three mottled-brown skinned bugs emerged, their golden leg and arm-wrappings a symbol of their office in the court of the queen. They stood apart, ignoring the pair, as a sleek Aldrassan emerged gracefully, her supple hairless skin a speckled red, her flowing silver gown trailing behind her. The wind seemed to have little effect on the material of her dress as she strode toward him, her arms outstretched.

She had six fingers on each slender hand.

"Guillermo March," she purred in a heavily accented Terran, her voice raised above the high-altitude wind and low hum of the hover-vehicle's engines atop the hospital. "It is good to finally meet the hero of Royal City."

Guillermo stood with arms folded before the statuesque attendant, a slight smile forming on his hardened face. A Terran would be able to see the roiling pain hidden behind the furrowed brow and hard-set mouth.

"I don't know about the word *hero*, ma'am," Guillermo shouted over the din. "I'm just a public servant who took down a drug lord. The motivation was to save my own people, actually. I guess I failed."

Out of the corner of his eye Guillermo noticed that Noob stood with her fists clenched, her arms crossed before her chest in a display of ceremonial readiness.

"Take a breather, will you Noob," Guillermo scolded. "You're embarrassing me."

The Aldrassan blinked her enormous black eyes,

lowered her arms to her sides and continued.

"I am Dlahuud, chief of the Queen's advisory committee, and I will be your escort today. Would you please follow me?"

Without waiting for an answer she spun on her heel and moved quickly to the waiting bat-shaped vehicle, its wings spread forward and up as if caught in mid-flight. A sudden gust of wind slightly ruffled Dlahuud's shimmering dress as she boarded, the dutiful bug aides climbing in after her. Reluctantly Guillermo climbed aboard, Noob quietly following, and the door whooshed shut behind them. Soon they faced Dlahuud on a u-shaped utilitarian couch within.

The wings of the craft swept back and in seconds the triangular roof of the hospital framed in the window became smaller and smaller, its landing lights slowly winking off. Dlahuud waved a hand at the bug pilot who began following his flight plan, passing swiftly over the rough crater of devastation below.

"Her majesty wants to assure you that we are all deeply sorry about the tragedy," she said, her small mouth a strange contrast to her large eyes. "And she has heard about the attempt on your life and is glad she could be of help. Your friend and former partner, as you know, is investigating the bombing, and soon we hope to discover the perpetrators of these heinous acts. It is her majesty's desire that we can soon bring an end to this horror and focus on rebuilding."

Guillermo flinched.

"I...really don't know what to say. I'm still trying to

process it."

"Of course," she said, her voice strangely calm. "It is the greatest of tragedies that the final remnant of Terrans, those courageous few who helped liberate the Five Rim worlds so long ago, have been sent to the Alatuud. Her majesty is terribly saddened by this tragic development. She wishes to speak to you personally, to comfort and aide you in this time of sadness. We are prepared to offer you any number of compensatory measures."

"Like what?"

"I have been instructed to see to your care and to transport you the palace so that you may gain audience with the Queen. The bodyguard is a simple gift from her majesty, and I hope that she has been adequate to your needs. Her majesty is eager to meet you, and is willing to help you find comfort for an event that is beyond anyone's capacity to understand. You are to be her honored guest for as long as you wish to stay."

Guillermo shifted in his seat.

"You have any luck finding any Terrans outside the city? In the jungles or marshes? Maybe living in the old New Titan enclave?"

He could see himself reflected in her huge black eyes as she sat silent for a moment. The soft hum of the engine could faintly be heard in the gloom. Noob might as well have been a statue placed next to him for decoration.

"Nothing yet," Dlahuud said finally. "We have not called off the search, even though the scanners have had negative results so far. We will search as long as you desire us to search, however. But perhaps I am speaking prematurely. Her majesty has some suggestions for how next to proceed, and it is my hope that you will agree with her prescription."

She smiled at him, the eerie thin teeth common to Aldrassans gleaming in the faint interior lighting, and then he turned to stare out the window.

They were fast approaching the palace.

The palace at Royal City was the second largest palace on the planet, the first being the ceremonial hive palace in the City of Knowledge, the traditional seat of power on the bug home world. That palace had long since been abandoned due to the dangerous radiation that emanated from it after an unfortunate accident that the conquering Terrans had used to their advantage. The "accident", planned meticulously by the invading Terrans, gave the Terrans the foothold they needed to conquer the bug home world so long ago. The Royal City palace was a collection of clustered red-brown spires that rose out of a massive chitinous base, the twenty-seven steeples glowing with thin blue lines of luminescence visible from over five kilometers away, even through the morning fog. It resembled a gigantic flower with long, slender pedals that reached far above the city, their placement seemingly random, resembling a sea urchin with curved and elongated spines. As their vehicle approached, more of the spires came into view, emerging from the humid mist like the talons of a predatory bird. The vehicle rapidly descended, and Guillermo felt the negative g-forces lift him out of his seat slightly. After weaving around a few of the spires which were lit from within by an eerie blue light, the vehicle found a landing pad surrounded by a vast crowd of bugs.

Dlahuud left her seat and entered the cockpit. She nudged the pilot.

When she returned, she adjusted her gown and then cleared her throat.

"The attempt on your life has revealed to the general populace that a Terran has indeed survived the attack. I cannot express the guilt that the public has felt at the destruction of the Terran enclave. There has been much protesting and unrest since the bombing, and her majesty's subjects who have gathered at the palace have done so in your honor. They are demanding answers for the death of the Terrans and also of their loved ones. The investigation is…going slowly."

"Forgive me, Chief Dlahuud," interrupted Noob. "Are you sure it is safe to land there? Have these citizens been screened?"

Guillermo cocked a smile at his new tag-along.

"All precautions have been taken, chamber guard," said Dlahuud calmly. "You may keep a vigilant watch on the crowd as we enter the palace."

Dlahuud turned to face Guillermo.

"I cannot stress enough the high honor it is for a non-native to be invited to the palace," said Dlahuud, that alien smile forming on her thin black lips. "You are one of a select few non-natives to be granted access."

"I feel special," Guillermo snorted. "Do you think I can get a souvenir?"

She gave him a sidelong look, her upper lip quivering

a bit.

"I suppose," she said, her big eyes blinking rapidly for a few seconds. "We can…arrange that if you like."

The transport ship floated slowly down to the platform, the wings extending up and forward again, and now Guillermo noticed a contingent of bugs standing at the ready with long spears, each tipped with a glowing gem that cast an eerie light on the insectoid faces of the crowd. As they emerged from the craft, there was a perplexing silence broken only by the occasional clicking of a mandible or the shuffling of a three toed foot. They walked along a path that opened in the crowd, the guards standing along the edges like living fence posts. Even though he had grown up around the silence that was bug communication, he still was unnerved by it sometimes.

Guillermo nudged Dlahuud with an elbow and she shot an uncomfortable glance at him.

"Are they excited I'm here? I can't really tell."

"Oh yes!" she exclaimed. "They are expressing their delight at seeing the last Terran —"

Suddenly a lone bug emerged from the crowd, sprinting toward Guillermo, a fist raised with something long and sharp barely visible. Guillermo started, his knees bent, the carbon fibers in his arm creaking, but out of the corner of his eye he saw a blur as Noob darted in front of him. She produced a small metallic rod that instantly extended into a long glaive that crackled with blue electricity, and in one motion severed the head of the attacking bug. As quick as she had moved she was again at his side, her glaive at the ready, her expressionless face scanning the crowd as the palace guards moved into place between the Terran and his escorts.

"What the crull?" he whispered.

"Quickly," Dlahuud muttered. "We must enter the palace immediately. This security threat is growing daily and her majesty believes that you are the key to peace."

Guillermo followed her, Noob holding her glaive and walking in reverse behind them as they entered the two massive chitin doors that swung out onto the landing platform.

The interior of the palace, a domain unseen by Terran eyes since the Phaedran Empire, was beautiful beyond Guillermo's ability to describe.

CHAPTER 7

Guillermo followed Dlahuud down a series of off-white, oval shaped corridors, bioluminescent gels spaced evenly along the high ceiling lighting their way. A hazy mist clouded the air, and he could feel the moisture on his skin as he proceeded. There was a musky odor that he did not recognize, something sour and pungent, like a mass of dead plant matter after it has been turned with a garden tool. Dlahuud walked gracefully ahead of him, her reddish mottled skin glistening with moisture, her shoulders swaying with each uncanny slow-motion stride. Noob walked calmly behind them, her stoic silence a mournful reminder of Guillermo's loneliness.

He made a mental note to change her name.

An entourage of bug attendants marched toward them down the corridor. They surrounded a smaller gold-skinned bug who wore black sleeves and leg coverings, an atlatl swinging from her hip, a uniquely slender rifle slung across her back. She stopped, and all of the other attendants followed her lead.

"Is this the Terran?" she chittered, her Terran mimicry high pitched like the buzzing of a bee near the ear. "I have wanted to speak with you for some time, Officer March."

Guillermo recognized the princess from the holo-vids of her various hunting escapades in the nearby marshes. She moved in, stood uncomfortably close to him, so close he could smell the pheromonal musk on her carapace. She reached out with one small hand and caressed his jawline. Guillermo tried not to cringe, furrowing his eyebrows instead.

"We are all terribly troubled by the business outside," she said as her entourage of guards and attendants surrounded them. "You are the last of your kind. It appears that someone is determined to erase your people from the universe. What do *you* think?"

Guillermo took one step back, placed his hand over his mouth, raised an eyebrow and said nothing.

"My mother is still on your side, you know."

"I guess…I'm glad of that," said Guillermo.

"When the bomb destroyed the Terran enclave, I felt the loss deeply. This is something difficult for my kind, emotion, but I do feel the absence of your race. It is… unfortunate."

She placed one small hand on his metallic arm, her small fingers caressing his wrist.

"Is this arm to your liking?" she asked.

"It'll do," he said. "I'm adjusting."

"Good," she said, moving away from him, her entourage following. "Perhaps we can go hunting sometime in the marshes. It is exhilarating."

He did not respond, only followed her with his eyes as she disappeared into the crowd of guards and attendants. He felt another hand on his arm and saw that Dlahuud was beckoning him forward, her small mouth forming a half-smile.

They moved on.

Soon the corridor widened into a chamber that was a nexus of seemingly unorganized passageways, all of them leading to an inevitable set of massive doors. The royal crest, to Guillermo a random series of raised slashes and orbs, decorated the doors with a golden inlay that reflected the bioluminescent light. Two red armored bugs stood on either side of the door, their ceremonial glaives at the ready. Noob knelt on the floor, her arms crossed before her chest, head bowed. Guillermo only cracked a wry smile at his bodyguard as Dlahuud turned to face him, her mouth a thin line.

"Stand here," she said, one palm extended toward him. "I have been informed that her majesty is meeting with the Council of Eight, an emergency meeting, something they are lately fond of doing. She will not be long."

Guillermo wondered how she had been informed

since he had been with her since they landed here, but he
assumed that she was wearing a subcutaneous
communicator. This kind of tech was common in the
upper class castes. The direct connection to the
Ontoccan Hegemony had its privileges, he supposed.

"I have all day," he said, his eyebrows raised, mouth
set. "I can't go back to my job until the doc gives me the
green light. I have as much time as needed, I figure."

She nodded at him, blinked her prodigious eyes, and
turned as the doors opened automatically, silently.
Beyond he saw another massive chamber, the walls and
floor coated with a shiny gold-flecked chitin that reflected
the light of several giant bioluminescent orbs hanging
from the ceiling far above. Each orb flickered with
millions of little fire-flies that hummed almost inaudibly.
The Queen sat on her radiant throne, various spindles of
chitinous fiber woven into an intricate pattern of artistic
glory rising up behind her padded seat. The trapezoidal,
stair-wrapped dais and the oriental fan-shaped throne
caused her to seem smaller than she appeared on the
holo-vids, cloaked in a gossamer golden ceremonial dress
that bespoke her station. Standing before her were seven
bugs, each of them of the blue-skinned ruling caste, and
they were silently moving, using their mystifying sign
language coupled with pheromonal cues.

Dlahuud stood to the side, her head bowed in
reverence, her six fingered hands locked together before
her waist. Noob remained motionless as if she dared not
look at the Queen.

Guillermo shuffled his feet just outside the doors, and

even though he could not understand much of the body language, he could indeed tell that the conversation was not pleasant. He noticed that several of them were displaying the signature vibrating head wag that he had experienced on the numerous occasions he had angered bugs in the past. It was a sign of irritation, of disagreement. This observation was also supported by the faintly sweet-and-sour aroma of frustration and anger.

He heard a few clicks of mandibles, and the seven bugs turned and strode toward him in a single file line, their hands balled into fists, arms stiff at their sides, their heads wagging rapidly as to sometimes blur their facial features. As they passed him a few stared at him, their mandibles clicking in agitation, a sign that usually denoted condescension. He watched them exit the antechamber, then turned back to face Dlahuud and let out a long breath.

"What's *their* problem?" he whispered.

"Officer Guillermo March," Dlahuud intoned, her voice taking on a musical quality. "I present the Twelfth Queen of Set Six, the mother of the Hive, Order of the Undying Luminescence - "

"Please," said the Queen, her mandibles clicking together to form a hissing version of Terran speech. "Don't bore him with all of those ceremonial titles, Dlahuud. He has been through enough already. And if we understand your profile you are a being who abhors formality."

"You got that right, your highness," said Guillermo, his eyes darting to the polished black floor, the gold flecks like stars in the void. He saw everyone's reflection in the floor which caused a vague state of vertigo. He raised his eyes to see the Queen descend the stairs, her gossamer train following her like the wings of a massive golden butterfly.

"You do not have to be afraid of us," she said. "We are your chief advocate as we have always been for the Terran enclave. We will do everything in our power to see that justice is served, that we find any other Terrans that may still be alive, and reunite you with them. Your former partner has been personally appointed by us to ensure swift justice for the Terrans and for my brood, even if he is being slowed by the incompetence of others."

"McFly?" Guillermo asked.

"This designation is not familiar to us, but if we are discussing your partner, then McFly it is."

"It's a pet name," Guillermo said. "Term of endearment. Guy's saved my skin a ton of times. You ever watch any pre-colony holo-vids? Like from the twentieth century? Great stuff, really."

The Queen stood silent, only shifting her gaze from Guillermo to Dlahuud.

"Perhaps we should keep to the matter at hand," said Dlahuud.

"Right...sorry," said Guillermo. "I suppose this is the part where you tell me everything is going to be fine, right?"

The Queen tilted her bulbous head.

"Of course not," she clicked. "We would never presume to understand your pain and loss. It is a difficult burden to bear for you, I know, but we want you to understand that you have the full backing of this government and of the Ontoccan Hegemony as well. A delegation is jumping here within the week to meet with the investigating officer's forensics team."

She moved closer, taking his mechanical hand in her small clawed fingers.

"We also regret that we could not provide a better replacement after the accident. Your injuries were extensive, and we had to use nanites to bond the robotic arm to your physiology. The genetic graft would not take for some reason, a flaw I could not remedy no matter my station or authority. You are simply not compatible."

He held her hand gently, not pulling away, surprised that his new hand did not flinch.

"Yeah," he said. "The doc explained it to me. Something about the degenerative nature of Terran DNA due to the organics in your atmosphere or whatever. I guess we pay for our sins."

"Forgive me, your majesty," said Dlahuud bowing at the waist. "Officer March, the medical team that revived you were some of the best in the Hegemony, and they worked diligently for some time to discover a way to remedy the DNA degradation problem. However, they were not able to successfully graft any of the re-grown tissues to your shoulder. They simply would not… take."

"Sure," said Guillermo as he let go of the Queen's hand. "I guess I'll just deal with what I've got. I've been having to do that a lot lately."

They were interrupted by the clicking of bug feet on

the chitinous floor as a green skinned soldier, a sizable
scar across his face, entered the throne room. He was
followed by several others of the same hue, their modified
Terran plasma rifles holstered on their backs. All of the
soldiers speedily locked into a line and knelt before the
Queen, their hands offered forward in a display of
submission, all but the grander bug in the center who
stood with only his scarred head bowed, his hands behind
his back.

The Queen waved her arms in greeting, and the taller
bug crossed his forearms in front of him and clicked them
together before wagging his head. The Queen silently
responded to him, and then gently touched Guillermo on
the shoulder.

"Forgive the general's rudeness, Officer March," she
chittered. "He has just informed me that the protests are
gaining strength in various quadrants of the city and
there are other protests forming in various other cities as
well. The military is very concerned about my safety, but
I have assured him that I am in no danger. He has been
listening to the Council of Eight again, even after I asked
him not bother with their hysteria."

The general clicked his mandibles together and then
uttered a vibrating hiss which caused the Queen to flinch
slightly.

"He is also concerned about my daughter who has
again left the palace on a hunt in the southern marshes."

Guillermo's lip twisted.

"Yeah, we met."

The Queen simply nodded but did not speak. There

was an awkward silence, common when bugs conversed.
He thought about the princess and how quickly she had
left him, her conversation terse and brief, common to a
politician on their way to more important matters.

"So the bombing happened, my race is gone, the
people are in a state of unrest, and she's out hunting?"
said Guillermo. "Kids these days."

"Indeed," offered the Queen. "My apologies if she has
offended you. I will instruct the general to retrieve her
immediately. She has not seen our perspective on
anything these past few months and it seems she has
taken to avoiding my presence with these hunting
expeditions. She is to take my place when I am gone, yet
she…embarrasses us."

The Queen, with a wave of her arm, dismissed the
soldiers who then filed out of the throne room, wasting
little time in doing her bidding. She then looked briefly at
Dlahuud, then turned back to face Guillermo.

"As stated before, the Hegemony delegation is on its
way from Ontocca as we speak. They should arrive
within the hour. There seems to be a shadow
organization working here on our world that we suspect
is led by some members of the Council of Eight, and I
fear they have also gained support within some of the
military caste. We assume that they desire to increase
their power over me, intending to wrest complete control
of the government for themselves. We cannot prove any
of this at present, as it is all…a feeling…but we are
hoping that we can give you the power you need to
discover the truth behind the bombing, the attack on the

hospital and other terrorist acts that have been occurring across the planet and in this very palace. Perhaps if you work together with your partner you can come to a more speedy conclusion."

"Yeah," said Guillermo, his lips pressing together briefly. "Once I can get together with McFly I'm sure we can turn this investigation around."

"Yes," said the Queen. "That would be good for all concerned."

She indicated her assistant with one small hand.

"Dlahuud will brief you on all information that we have been able to glean. I want you to join…McFly's… efforts regardless of what your supervisors plan for you. However, we are asking for your help because there have been two attempts on our life since the bombing occurred, attempts made by attendants who were, until their betrayal, completely loyal to my house. This is the reason for the general's hasty interruption of our meeting."

"So somebody doesn't like that you were so friendly to us?" mused Guillermo. "That figures. If I'm going to be working for you then I need some assurances."

The queen paused and Guillermo could see his reflection in both of her large compound eyes. She looked at Dlahuud and nodded, and the Aldrassan began to close the huge double doors to the throne room. Noob remained on her knees, passing out of view once the doors quietly closed.

The Queen clasped her hands calmly before her tiny waist.

"We are thinking," Dlahuud explained. "That these attacks are the work of a terrorist organization that we feel may be attached somehow to the Council of Eight. McFly has, as we understand, desired to discuss this with you further, but the information he has uncovered is apparently of an extremely delicate matter, information he will not discuss fully even with us. Her majesty will insure your safety and the use of her personal guard if you will promise to keep her majesty informed as to what McFly has discovered."

Dlahuud touched Guillermo's mechanical arm then, and he chuckled a bit in surprise at the sudden feeling of her soft hand, the nanites finally registering the sense.

"It's about time," he said, and after seeing the Queen tilt her head his face became grave. He felt uncomfortable, sure that even though the Queen had always been a supporter of Terran causes, something in her assistant's tone threw him off.

"Sorry," he said, trying to mask his suspicion. "My arm. I get a little feeling back a bit at a time. Bad timing, I guess. Look. It doesn't matter if I have support from the security force. I brought down Death Adder without them…I suppose what I'm saying is that if you get me clearance I'll get to the bottom of this. I have ways of getting information that McFly will never be able to access. Besides, he may just tell me everything once we can get together."

"Time is, as your kind says, of the essence," said Dlahuud, her eyes reflecting his face. "We are sure that because of your relationship with McFly he will be cooperative in working with you. Tell him that our operatives have been informing us that the plans for the bombing had been in motion years before, that someone is plotting the destruction of the royal family, possibly a coup. We have been aware of some form of shadow group for some time, and currently we are at a loss to discover their means or their origins. If there is anything you need, we will be happy to provide it."

Guillermo blinked. Dlahuud and the Queen shared a brief glance.

"Has my chamber guard pleased you?" asked the Queen. "She was a gift to you, to ensure your safety. She is highly capable of anything you might require of her."

"She's out there groveling right now, your highness," Guillermo said. "Does she really have to do that?"

"It is bred into her from birth," offered the Queen. "Conditioned to be the servant of whomever we desire, and utterly effective at ensuring the safety of her charge. She is the product of the unfortunate breeding experiments perpetrated by your ancestors, but her kind are used for more noble purposes since the fall of the Empire. Her talents are far more than you realize."

Dlahuud pulled on the door to reveal Noob kneeling before them, her arms crossed before her chest, her head bowed in reverence.

"She will not disobey her orders, Officer March," said the Queen, the slight breeze from the door fluttering her gossamer gown. "I trust you will not dishonor her purpose."

Guillermo, cowing to custom, bowed slightly at the

waist and smiled.

"Certainly not, your majesty. I'll keep her out of trouble."

CHAPTER 8

It took the better part of the next day for Guillermo to be cleared for duty even though the Queen's officials did their best to fight through the red tape it required. The hospital's chief cyberneticist, a Fraaz named Yeep, hung from the balcony window of Guillermo's guest room resembling a great winged fox with black fur. Yeep used the fingers on the ends of his leathery wings to manipulate an electromagnetic probe, poking uncomfortably at the joints on Guillermo's mechanical arm.

"Stop moving, please," he said, his gravelly voice tinged with deep tones and high pitched whistles. "It will only take a few more moments."

Guillermo had only seen a few of Yeep's species, but this Ontocca-born Fraaz seemed more agreeable than most. The Phaedran Empire had made an example of them during the rebellion, reducing their home planet to a nuclear wasteland. All known Fraaz hailed from Ontocca at present, and none of them understood Terran cultural cues at all.

"How soon can I get back to work, Doc? I have

criminals to bust."

"I assume you are not saying you are inflating them, Officer March," said Yeep, his small purple eyes blinking rapidly behind thick polarized goggles.

Fraaz did not see very well in bright light.

"Of course not, Doc," said Guillermo, wincing a bit when Yeep tapped the probe to his index finger, a small spark flickering there. "You about done?"

Yeep dropped the probe to his open tool kit on Guillermo's lap and then fluttered to the chitin floor of the balcony, his wings tucked up so that he awkwardly propped himself up on all fours. He looked at Guillermo, the lenses in his goggles whirring and adjusting to the ambient light in the room.

"All done," he said. "I will communicate this to your superiors immediately. Get you back to work."

"Good," said Guillermo, flexing his mechanical fingers and then making a fist. "For what it's worth, thanks."

"Glad to be of service, Guillermo. The feeling should continue to increase over time. Be patient with the process. And please do not task the arm. It was a puzzle to attach it to your anatomy properly."

"Thanks," said Guillermo. "I'll try."

Yeep jumped a few feet off the floor then, his great leathery wings unfurling to stir the air in the room, a faint yet pungent musk on the artificial breeze he created as he ascended. Yeep closed his tool kit with his foot, grabbed it with the other and then dove over the balcony railing. Guillermo rose to see Yeep glide on the thermal drafts coming in from the tropical forest outside the city, and then spiral gracefully out of view. A Fraaz's true element was air.

Guillermo's communicator band flickered to life and produced a staticky image of McFly.

"Is this line secure?" asked McFly.

"Encode," Guillermo replied. "Now it is. A little gift from our friend the Queen. Much better than the other model I used to have."

McFly stared into the emitter on his end, the image flickering for a moment. He seemed to pause at the mention of the Queen.

"You ready for that bottle of aavriil?" McFly asked finally.

"Thought you'd never ask."

"Excellent," said McFly, his mandibles clicking away. "I am at my residence. Please use your communicator when you arrive at my door. I will let you in. I am to testify before the security chief tomorrow and I want to run some things by you before I prepare my statement. I have discovered some…discrepancies, and to use our metaphor, this bottle of aavriil is of a particularly interesting flavor. Anyway, as I said, I will let you in when you let me know that you are outside my door."

"See you there."

The image winked out and Guillermo exited his room to find Noob standing stoically outside the door.

"Going to visit my old partner McFly," said Guillermo. "You coming?"

"I am bound to your service, sir," chittered the bug. "I go where you go."

"Then don't fall behind."

Noob followed Guillermo into the nearest lift tube
where they began their descent to the hangar bay. After a
moment the lift tube doors swished open and they exited
onto the vast interior tarmac, an open hole to the city
beyond letting little shafts of light fall across them
through the clouds. Guillermo was looking for some
transportation and hopefully a little freedom.

Dlahuud spun to face them, and Guillermo waved at
her and approached. She walked calmly to greet them,
her smile full of strange narrow teeth.

"Guillermo," she said softly. "I hope I may call you by
your first name. Is this proper?"

"Whatever, Dlahuud. I don't have a preference. I'm
not even a real cop anymore."

"Soon you will be reinstated. Her majesty wanted
you to have something to help you with your
investigation, so she has ordered a new hover-bike for
you. Take your pick from the motor pool. Simply
produce this chip to the tech. He is currently running
diagnostics at the moment and is expecting you."

She gave him a small yellow disc that looked like a
plastic coin and he palmed it. Mechanically, she pointed
one slender finger toward a line of hover-bikes, each
sitting in their docking clamps. A short, slender bug
crouched near one of them, an open red tool box near his
feet.

Guillermo cracked a smile at Dlahuud as she scurried
away, then he walked calmly to the row of bikes. The
mechanic didn't seem notice him, busy using a sonic

resonator on the fusion coils, so Guillermo blew a heavy breath his way.

The bug jumped up, spun around, his hyper-sensitive olfactory system overloaded with Terran bad breath. The mechanic nodded, his mandibles clicking but not producing Terran speech, and then motioned with one small hand for the two of them to follow. He lead them to a larger hover bike moored in two sets of docking clamps. The mechanic moved his clawed fingers over the control studs and the bike's actuators awoke with a low hum. Guillermo read the hieroglyphs which stated that the bike was requiring a voice activation.

"Guillermo March," he said, leaning close to the steering bars, and the bike's engine roared to life. He hopped aboard, feeling the familiar vibration of the fusion engine as it began to harmlessly emit small bolts of static that explored the chitinous landing pad beneath it like glowing fingers. The mechanic produced a small hand-held device that he manipulated with his nimble fingers, remotely releasing the docking clamps so that Guillermo could begin pre-flight checks that burned only seconds.

All systems were perfectly ready to go. Guillermo glanced at Noob.

"You should probably get your own bike because I don't share. No offense."

Noob silently boarded her own bike and quietly activated the engine, revving it a few times before nodding her head and hissing.

"Got it," replied Guillermo.

He pushed the throttle up and rose above the tarmac,

then rocketed out of the hangar bay with Noob hot on his heels. He used the navigation screen to line up with traffic, the bike utilizing an algorithm that accessed global positioning software and probability engines to ensure that his journey was accident free. He made a mental note to disable that as soon as he could. He roared to the southern residential district, a modest canyon of high-rise apartments and domiciles, to McFly's current address, living alone on his meager security force salary.

After some unceremonious aerial acrobatics, Guillermo and Noob reached the roof of McFly's apartment building only to find that all of the spaces were filled with vehicles which left zero room for parking their bikes. Guillermo breathed more Guajiin profanity as he realized that he would have to descend into the much seedier lower levels.

He wished he had spent some time working on his bike's security protocols.

With a motion of his hand, they spiraled down between the gargantuan grey towers, their engines echoing from the layers of balconies that lined the outer walls of the buildings like a duracrete layer cake. As they dropped down and down they watched the filth increase in thickness, as it was the lower castes who lived on these deeper levels. They would be parking on the street far below, riding the lift to the top, and hoping that some young gang member didn't steal their bikes or cannibalize it for parts or even siphon the emitter fluid for a cheap yet dangerous high.

As they approached the ground the darkness

enveloped them. Several bioluminescent street lamps, those that were not hanging loose and desiccated, emitted jagged puddles of light here and there. The emitters on the underside of their bikes arced blue lightening that pushed away a few plastic containers left on the street. They landed in deathly silence, but just as they did there was movement at the edge of Guillermo's vision that caused him to sit quietly on his bike without dismounting.

He waited, but nothing else came into view.

He decided to try and convince Noob to stay with the horses.

"But I must assure your safety at all times," Noob protested.

"I think I can take care of myself in this dive. The apartment is just a few floors up, like thirty. Nobody's expecting me to be here. If I get in trouble I'll call you on the comm. Got it?"

"I must protest," Noob clicked. "If I allow you to come to harm I will be honor bound to take my own life."

Guillermo placed his mechanical hand on her thickly armored shoulder.

"I promise I won't be long. Don't go killing yourself just yet. If you follow me I'll change your name again. Something more humiliating."

"This word you call me is humiliating? Why would you do that?"

With a wry smile he backed away, then turned and walked to the massive center pillar of the building. He passed a small, dimly lit j'umaa shop where a battered old bug stood just outside the door wiping out a greasy cup with a dirty rag. Guillermo nodded at the shopkeep, and the bug turned and went back into the empty cafe to a cluster of stained tables dimly lit by a flickering overhead lamp. He made his way to a lift embedded in the center strut of the building's five support pillars, rode it up thirty levels to his partner's floor, then exited into a hexagonal hallway that Guillermo always felt needed some paint and a few plants.

The whole lower half of the building needed repairs, but bugs were not interested in repairing things that were not immediately inoperable, and interior decoration was not on the list at all.

He arrived at McFly's apartment, noticed a few scratches in the paint, and the crooked number on the door. He looked at his communication band and muttered a seven digit code that called McFly's comm. The small holographic emitter winked on and a tiny three dimensional image of a green bell wiggled above his wrist.

He now regretted not reading the instruction file that came with the comm band. He was pretty sure this was a default feature that could be modified to not be so obvious...or noisy. It continued to ring, and he felt strange standing in this hallway, hoping no one would exit their apartment and see him standing outside the door like some kind of sad salesman.

He decided to knock, but as he did the communicator continued to ring, and no matter how many commands he uttered, he couldn't manage to make it stop.

He really should have read the instruction file.

He rapped on the door with his metal hand, the image

of the little green bell wiggling uncontrollably. This frustrated him so much that he rapped a little too hard and left a small knuckle-shaped dent in the door, the sound of it a little too loud in this echoing hallway. His eyebrows raised when he found zero damage on his knuckles.

A door whooshed open down the hall and a small bug child peeked around the doorframe. The child clicked a lower mandible, then went back inside and the door swished shut.

This was getting embarrassing.

The bell continued to ring until finally an image of McFly appeared in transparent green holographic form floating above Guillermo's wrist. An automated message ran across McFly's chest and shoulders: "The Special Investigator is not answering at the moment. Please leave a message and he will return your call as soon as he is able. Thank you."

"You called me, McFly, old buddy," he began, then there was a beep which meant that now Guillermo would have to record a message.

He cleared his throat, then repeated.

"I said…you called me, partner," he said, his voice strained with frustration. "I guess you must have stepped out or whatever. I'll be down at the j'umaa shop at street level if you want to meet. I'll come back up here in an hour."

He turned, accidentally figuring out that if he waved his hand over the communicator band it would shut off, granting him some normalcy. When he began to walk

away from the door he heard a slight noise from inside
the apartment, a shifting of something heavy, and that
caused the little hairs to stand up on the back of his neck.
He faced the door again, pounding on it this time with his
natural born fist, slamming away at the new dent he had
created, the little chips of paint flaking from the almond-
shaped divot.

He raised his left wrist again and thought about
calling the station. He still had the number memorized,
but after saying "security station" the little bell appeared
again. In moments an image floated before him of a
dispatch tech, a female bug he'd named Nancy who he
was thankful spoke Terran.

"Guillermo," she said. "So good to see you up and
around. How are you?"

"No time for the usual chat, Nancy. Do you have a
way to get me into McFly's place? Override the security
protocol?"

"Sure, but why?"

"I need in there. I got a bad feeling. It's probably
nothing. Just do it...now."

He heard the magnetic lock click and then whirr, and
then the door irised open. He could feel a warm breeze
as the room depressurized. McFly liked to keep the
environmental systems humid in his apartment because
he grew up in the marshes, not in the city. He once said
that it helped him think when he needed to figure out a
case.

The foyer was as tidy as the living area, and
Guillermo moved cautiously through the apartment, his

grey eyes scanning the room, his hands at the ready as he had not been issued a weapon as yet. He was still waiting for the doc to turn in the clearance forms, but now he wished he had waited as the eerie silence of the apartment began to close in around his mind like clear plastic over his face, asphyxiating his resolve.

There was a strange smell.

He moved through the kitchen, a pot of boiling broth bubbling and roiling, the acrid odor of rotting vegetables in the liquid fluttering and dancing. He switched off the burner and turned to face a steamed over window, the condensation collecting in a small trough at the bottom of the sash. He had never been able to get used to bug cooking, most of it consisting broths and sugary syrups that did not digest well in a Terran stomach. Some of their food caused hallucinations in Terrans.

Still no sign of McFly.

His eye found the long hallway that led to the bedroom and the small study that McFly often used to gather his thoughts, to work through evidence, to generally show him up most days during the early months of their career together, back before he had to go undercover and become a rogue. He found his way past the study, noticing that the two holo-vids that usually flickered with data and various manipulative images were completely dark, the emitter orbs two lifeless eyes staring back at him.

"Guillermo are you still there?"

He did his best not to jump when Nancy's voice chittered over his communicator band, but he failed miserably.

He let out a long breath.

Getting weak, Guillermo.

"Yeah, Nancy old girl. Still here. McFly say anything about stepping out for a bite or whatever? He left the burner going on the stove."

There was a strange pause.

"Not to my knowledge."

As he disconnected the comm, he crept toward the back bedroom, the eerie quiet of the hallway somehow weighing on his back like the heavy pack he was forced to carry during academy training. He turned his head slightly and a long shadow fell across the wall. He spun to face Noob who stood just visible in the kitchen, her collapsible electro-glaive in one hand. She shook it once and it extended out to its full length and a cluster of sparks burst from the razor-sharp business end.

"Noob," Guillermo growled. "I told you to wait with the bikes. If you are bound to my service, then why don't you crulling *serve* me?"

The bug took one step forward, her head shaking side to side.

"Sir," she said calmly. "There is a curious odor at the end of the hall. It is of burned flesh."

Guillermo turned, stalked down the hall, through the bedroom. He noticed a barely perceptible layer of grey smoke floating just near the ceiling. The bedroom was in disarray, the hammock that McFly and his kind used as a bed had been severed at one end and lay stretched on the floor like a fishing net. His wardrobe had been knocked over and the contents strewn around the room in uneven patterns. The mimic box McFly had used to perfect his Terran lay on its side, the crystalline holo-emitter shattered.

The bathroom door was closed.

Guillermo moved to the lavatory door, activated the motion sensor on the side and found it to be locked. Noob appeared at the bedroom door, her glaive collapsing into a small rod which she quickly tucked away in her belt pouch.

"We must open the door," Noob said.

"Yeah, obviously," growled Guillermo. "Looks like its been locked from the inside. I don't like this at all."

"Should we call the authorities?"

"I have to know…before the bureaucrats get involved."

Guillermo began to knock on the bathroom door, then began pounding on it with his metallic fist, and after nearly denting it realized that it probably would have difficulty opening if it were warped as it was designed to slide into a perpendicular slot in the wall.

Guillermo placed his hands on his hips and bowed his head, let out a breath, and Noob produced a small tool from her belt and crouched near the door, popped a panel on the wall and began poking around on a console within. Soon there was a click and a magnetic hum and the door popped open just a millimeter and a new gout of smoke bellowed into the room.

"What the chert is that?" coughed Guillermo as he placed his metallic fingers into the crevice and pulled.

Inside lay McFly's lifeless body, a plasma burned hole in one eye and his personal plasma pistol in one rigid fist.

Guillermo bowed his head, pushing the doorway further open in rage, listening to the servos in the door fail and crack.

"This is now a crime scene, Noob," Guillermo managed, backing away into the bedroom and standing near the upturned wardrobe. "We have to call it in."

Noob only knelt in the floor outside the bathroom, her hands raised in ceremonial respect for the dead.

"Or I'll call it in," said Guillermo, his eyes rolling. "You just do whatever it is you do when your kind dies."

He spoke his communicator band to life and dialed up Nancy again. She took the news worse than Noob.

CHAPTER 9

The crowd had begun to form in the street outside McFly's apartment tower within hours of his death was leaked by a neighbor, the sea of bugs swelling by the minute. They carried hieroglyphic signs accusing the government of a conspiracy, some of them demanding that the monarchy be fully empowered. Their growing numbers made the investigation a difficult task in that a majority of security force personnel had to act as perimeter guards to keep onlookers, and some media, from intruding on the crime scene, not to mention tracking down the digital culprit who had posted the news and made all of their jobs that much harder.

Guillermo stood in the middle of McFly's apartment, his grey eyes moving slowly about the room. The forensics team scanned every inch of the floor, walls and ceiling as they catalogued every microscopic fiber and residue. It wasn't long before chief examiner Victor arrived, his quiet demeanor the opposite of what Guillermo knew to be true.

Victor, from the beginning, had been a thorn in Guillermo's side. Because of this, the name he had given him when mouthed looked like "Victor", but he actually always said the word "sphincter".

To Guillermo's knowledge, Victor had never caught on.

"Officer March," clicked Victor as he sidled up to him, uncomfortably close. "I will be needing a full statement from you soon. Don't go anywhere."

"I'm not the criminal here," said Guillermo, his eyes staring at Victor's badge. "I'll get reinstated as soon as Doc Yeep fills out the forms. Then I'll be on this case like a shad-tick on an eldritch rat."

Victor produced a shiny metal object and a plasma pistol and then handed it to Guillermo unceremoniously.

"It has already happened, much to my dismay," he chittered. "I do not know why the Queen has requested the reinstatement of such a reckless officer, but it is not my decision to make. Now please exit the room so that we might work to find the truth of what happened here. You can retrieve your weapon when you report to the station."

Guillermo did not take time to look at the badge,

handing it over to Noob who simply turned it over in her slender hand, made a motion to ask Guillermo why she should hold it, then dutifully placed it in her belt pouch. Guillermo strapped the concealed holster around his shoulder, fidgeting with the magnetic clasps, his blood boiling.

"Well it wasn't a suicide if that's what you're wondering," growled Guillermo. "I've known McFly a long time and he wasn't the suicidal type. Somebody thought he knew too much about something and killed him."

"Do you know this for certain? Did you witness the inspector's death? Perhaps you want to change the story that you gave my lieutenant."

Guillermo let out a strained breath.

"No, you little beetle, I don't. McFly said that someone was following him, that he was in danger because of something he had discovered. He was about to tell me what that was, asked me here over the comm, but he was really paranoid about it."

Victor raised his wrist, tapped on a small emitter with a clawed finger, and an image emerged of McFly, a chrono flashing near the dead detective's holographic left shoulder indicating that the message was sent only hours ago. There was a crackle of static and McFly's body language began registering, interpreted and spelled out at the bottom of the image in hieroglyphs.

"I have betrayed my Queen," it read. "The avriil is hidden in the normal place. If you get this message then it means I have been found out. I am afraid I cannot go on living knowing what I know about the upper caste. War is imminent."

The image froze for a second as a line of green static washed from McFly's shoulders to the top of his head.

"Forgive me," he continued. "I am…I am dreadfully sorry…"

The image faintly caught the shape of the barrel of a plasma pistol in the top right corner before the image was cut off abruptly.

"That doesn't prove anything," Guillermo said. "Images can be altered so easily. There's no way he killed himself."

Victor pulled a small device from a pouch strapped to his waist. He thumbed it awake and began typing away on it as if ignoring Guillermo.

"The pistol in his hand was encoded to him," said Victor. "It is impossible to be operated by anyone but the inspector. I am therefore ruling it a suicide at the moment. Anything else at this time would be conjecture. It is obvious he was planning to take his life."

"If there's any conjecture, sphincter," said Guillermo. "It's that this video is crulling false. He told me he was being watched. He knew something. Something about the bombing, who was behind it, but he was silenced."

"Silenced?"

"Yeah," said Guillermo, his eyes dancing from the floor to Victor's little square communication device. "But you're too dull to figure this out. Somewhere in this apartment is some kind of evidence pointing to what McFly knew, that is if you haven't buried it already."

"I would never hide evidence, Officer March. There is no need to lecture me."

Just then a stocky little bug approached, his body language and pheromones telling Victor something Guillermo figured was important. Victor chittered something unintelligible and then turned and faced Guillermo.

"You must leave the room now," he said mechanically. "Please report directly to the security station near the lift and I will be visiting you shortly to tie off any loose ends. This case is, as you used to say, cut and dried…but we will look for anything suspicious, of course."

Guillermo puffed out his chest and Noob placed a small hand on his shoulder. Guillermo glared at her hand until she removed it.

"You are completely out of your insectoid brain if you think I'm going to sit idly by and let some guy who didn't give a leech-worm in an Ontoccan sandstorm about McFly in the first place."

The chief examiner cocked his head to the side.

"I am sorry you were emotionally attached to the detective. Violent outbursts will not bring him back or further the progress in the case of his death. Shall I remind you that I outrank you? Please exit into the hallway immediately or I will have you escorted there."

Guillermo turned a bright shade of red, puffed out his lips, and then he felt the firm hand of Noob grab his arm and gently tug.

"It would be best if we leave, sir," she offered. "We must report to the Queen and let her know of our progress."

He turned his head toward her as if in slow motion.

"Sure," he growled. "I suppose we should. We can tell her we are getting nowhere."

He then purposefully faced away from Victor.

"This low-life v'oshtu is such a waste of air," he said. "I don't know why he's been assigned to the case instead of someone more…I don't know…not dirty."

"He looks clean to me, sir," said Noob.

"I'll tell you later."

After more security forces arrived, Guillermo followed Noob out of the apartment, down the crowded hall and then jumped into the lift before the security officers could detain them. They rode down a few floors until an elderly bug exited, leaving them alone in the little square box. This is when Noob popped the metallic panel just beneath the controls and halted the lift between floors. She turned to face Guillermo.

"He is lying," she clicked. "What do you need me to do."

"He's lying? Tell me something I don't know. That whole recording of McFly was rigged."

She placed a hand on his arm.

"No," she said. "The chief examiner. He is lying about knowing that the recording is a fake. I am able to read him, something I have been trained to do in service of her majesty. The chief examiner knows the recording has been altered."

She turned, pressed the button that re-engaged the lift, and closed the panel quietly.

"Well then we have to get back into that apartment and take a look around," Guillermo said. "How do you suppose we do that with sphincter's goons crawling all over it?"

"Leave that to me, sir," she said as the doors opened on the crowded street. "I will devise a way in."

Guillermo's blood percolated with deep anger, his mind reeling at the idea that Victor's men might be tampering with evidence as they stood down here wasting precious time. His mechanical arm twitched as the neurons fired haphazardly through the artificial nerve clusters, his rage widening his eyes, his teeth gritting together at the thought of his partner's unjust murder.

The crowd was thick, and the security forces were trying to clear an area around the doors to the lift but were not doing a very good job of it. Guillermo pushed forward, but stopped when four of the protestors forced their way toward him. One of the protestors, a brown skinned working class bug, grabbed the arm of one of the security force troops while the others tried to rout the crowd, shoving him to the ground. Guillermo was on the first one before he could think about it, his arm pounding at the face of the protestor. Another protestor grabbed at Guillermo's other arm and he brought his elbow back into his throat, then shifted his weight and dropped his shoulder onto the chest of the first protestor. The security force troop scooted away from the melee on his back, reaching for his shock-baton with a trembling clawed hand.

Guillermo kicked at the first protestor, ignoring the

blows of the other while pounding away at the compound
eyes and clicking mandibles of the first, and the security
force rushed forward to drag Guillermo away from the
protestors who limped or crawled away in fear of the
angry Terran. The security force troops helped Guillermo
to his feet, two of them awkwardly but genuinely patting
him on the back, one of them chittering in broken Terran:
"Thank's Officer Maaarrrrgghch."

But he ignored them, his shoulders rising and falling
as he seethed, his grey eyes staring from beneath
furrowed brows, his fists clenching and releasing, and
then he felt the gentle hand of Noob on his shoulder.

He flinched, shaking her hand off of him.

"Perhaps you should come with me, Guillermo," she
said. "Abusing the locals will not bring your friend back
or allow you to investigate his murder officially."

He turned to face her, his eyes narrowing, but
somehow he had relieved the tension, focused it
elsewhere even if his motives were not pure.

"Sure," he said as he spied the j'umaa cafe nearby.
"But first I have to have a drink."

CHAPTER 10

"I hope they haven't scrubbed all of the evidence,"
said Guillermo. "You said sphincter was lying?"

"Yes," said Noob as she stared out the window of the
j'umaa shop, watching as night fell upon the street
outside, the darkness becoming more and more palpable.

"Since he is lying about the video, he probably knows more about your friend's death than he is willing to tell."

Guillermo stared blankly out the window as well, watching as the aging street lights outside fought to push back the encroaching velvet dark. Night at the lower levels of the city were inky black. He remembered hiding out at street level when he was undercover, how the strange became stranger down here, the very atmosphere sucking the life out of all of the destitute beings who resided here.

A couple of security officers had come to the cafe to question Guillermo about the call he had received earlier in the day and then it turned into a rather accusatory inquisition when they began grilling him about the altercation with the protestors. He smiled through the entire interview, nodding and laughing at the most annoying moments while Noob sat stoically across the table from him, the jokes not seeming to register with her.

He had taken what he needed from the fight and wasn't ashamed at all.

Shortly after the security force officers left he had entered a code on his communicator band and placed a call to an old friend, a restauranteur of sorts, but the conversation was brief and cryptic. He spread the sarcasm thick, spoke in code, and insisted that his old friend be "ready to fry up some gornak steaks."

Noob appeared to ignore him.

After most of the patrons had left, they sat watching the crowd of protestors slowly begin to disperse as night fell on the neighborhood. After a while there were only a few protestors and then only security forces, and then only a token pair of guards. Noob tapped on the plasteel window beside their booth, rose, and then stood beside Guillermo. She leaned forward and placed her slender hands on the table and spread her clawed fingers.

"We should go," she said. "It is time."

Guillermo bounced three chids on the table and they slowly walked toward the back exit as planned and then down a long alleyway. The alley was actually a long tunnel that ran through the towering building to allow delivery trucks to access the cafe from the street outside. The two of them trotted along in the darkness, Guillermo following Noob's soft footfalls because his vision was nearly useless in the jet-black metallic tube.

As they emerged from the tunnel a misty humid breeze caressed his face and he could see the faint glow of the security lights near the entrance to McFly's apartment building. Noob jogged ahead of him, darting toward one of the massive support pillars, her form low to the ground, and before he could speak she leaped a meter into the air and clung to the side of the duracrete pillar. She produced a small silver device, something like a tiny pistol, and with a sound like a puff of compressed air a cord shot out of it and dangled just within Guillermo's reach.

"Can you climb?" she asked, her Terran mimicry of speech faint.

"How did you…I mean how can you stick to the wall like that?"

"Your people bred chamber guards for a more secret

purpose long ago," she chittered quietly. "Now climb."

He acknowledged her silently, gripping the sticky white cord, placing one boot in a slight crease etched into the pillar.

She began to ascend the side of the building, her hands and feet clinging to the duracrete like a spider, and remarkably she was able to hold his weight as he pulled himself along. The bugs, although most times considered to be his self-confessed greatest annoyance, managed to surprise him once in a while.

The gun attached to her belt squeaked and fed out more line as they climbed, adjusting to his weight, and she hugged the side of the apartment building to give herself more leverage as she ascended. Guillermo began to wonder what other talents she possessed and was also very glad she was on his side so far. He made a mental note not to blow it.

The adhesive quality of the cord allowed Guillermo to hold on rather easily. Noob continued to climb silently along the horizontal grooves of the wall until she reached the outside window of McFly's apartment, the soft glow from within reflected in her great compound eyes.

"I have found it, Officer March," she said, not looking down at him. "It appears to be vacant. How are you progressing?"

Guillermo could feel the strain on his mechanical arm, an unwelcome tingling sensation that reached down into his chest cavity and wrenched his bones and three of his ribs. He didn't think rappelling was in the arm's design.

"I'm fine," he coughed. "Do you think you can get

in?"

She paused, her right hand reaching for a small cylindrical object on her belt.

"I am confident that I will succeed," she said, and a small blue flame appeared. Little molten flecks of plasteel fell from the window, stinging his exposed skin, but not enough for him to complain.

She put the little torch away and then pressed in on the window, and before long she was slithering inside. He soon began rising toward the window, the cord being drawn up into the new opening. He came closer, could see the cooling edge of the plasteel that had been cut away, and he began to reach with his metal fingers for the hole.

The cord stopped.

He heard a noise from inside the apartment, something breaking, and the cord jerked once. Frantically he began to climb it, but his feet couldn't gain purchase on the slippery wall and something inside his head screamed about how Noob had made it look so easy.

He tried not to look down, looked down, gasped, then looked at the opening.

He reached for the edge, his metallic fingers grasping at the window, and just as he managed to get three of his fingertips locked on the sill the cord went slack. The metal strained in his arm as he pulled himself up and grabbed on with his other hand. He was able to hoist himself higher, just enough to see inside the dimly lit apartment.

Noob was a blur of movement, whirling and flashing

her electro-glaive, frantically fighting someone he could not see.

"Noob!" he shouted, and then something knocked her down, something that looked like a jagged shadow.

His muscles strained as he pulled himself higher, getting his torso through the window, feeling the edge of the plasteel dig into his stomach, cut his fleshy fingers, and he could smell blood. Something moved in the room, banging against a table and sending it flying. He rolled over into the apartment, bitterly glad for the solid floor beneath his face as he smacked his cheek bone onto it. Before he could get to his knees and grab his pistol something brushed past him, and then he felt a crushing grip on his wrist as he was thrown to the floor, but he grunted to a sitting position and then fumbled for the pistol.

He could hear deep breathing, but he saw nothing but a darkened apartment.

He whipped out the pistol and sprung to his feet, pointing it at nothing in particular. He didn't see the attacker, but he saw Noob rise from the floor a few meters away, her electro-glaive snapping out to its full length, the curved silver blade crackling with energy. She shook her head in frustration, then slashed at the air and briefly Guillermo caught the edge of a silhouette, something humanoid, a faint glimmer of black armor that deflected her glaive with only a tell-tale shower of sparks. Then he was stung by a painful blow to the chest which knocked him across the room and over a table.

He rolled to his feet, stood, and as quick as he could

manage he fired a shot at the silhouette, but it bounced away, and as Noob raised her glaive again, a red light brightened the room and dissolved a molten hole, the edges dripping with molten slag. There was a blast of hot air that knocked both of them to the floor and he could hear the sound of something like an engine that faded on the wind. As he rose to his feet again he noticed Noob collapsing to the floor, holding her side.

He rushed to her, but she held one hand out in protest, and in the gloom he could see that she had suffered a monstrous slashing wound to the abdomen. Guillermo had never seen so much bug blood. It was the lightest shade of fluorescent green.

"I'll get help," he stammered. "Don't die on me."

She sputtered out a couple of syllables, but couldn't manage to speak Terran under such duress. Holstering his pistol, he called up the security force precinct and his communicator fired to life, and in seconds there was the familiar voice of Nancy, the dispatch operator.

"Guillermo," she said. "Are you calling from…you're not supposed to be there."

"Yeah, yeah," he growled. "I have an emergency. I need an immediate med-flight from the outside window of McFly's apartment. If you don't get here soon, we'll lose her."

"Who?"

"Never mind! Just get here!"

He waved a hand over his wrist, cutting off the transmission, then took Noob's limp hand in his, and noticed some of the fluid had begun to leak from her mouth.

"Look at me, tough old girl," he said. "I take back everything I said about you. You have to pull through."

She was unresponsive, but he could see that she was still breathing.

"Look," he said, his voice shaky. "I'm sorry I named you Noob. You fought bravely, and for what? Me? I'm totally not worth it...last Terran or not. I think you deserve a better name...like...I don't know...Dervish. Yeah. Dervish is much more honorable."

She coughed, spitting some of the fluid on his shirt, and he could see that he was now being soaked in it, the floor aglow with Dervish's lifeblood. She raised one fist and pressed it against his chest, and it took him a few moments to realize that she was trying to hand him something, but in her weakened state missed his hand.

He opened her nearly limp fingers and found a small rectangular data card.

"Took it," she chittered, fluid oozing from her mouth. "F-f-f-f-rrom...". And then she fell limp in his arms as the low sound of sirens approached. In moments a medi-flight vehicle hovered just outside the gaping hole in the wall, its engines causing the detritus to fly about the room, the green and blue lights flashing and strobing around the small apartment.

As the med-techs moved in and Guillermo backed away, watching them try to stabilize her with lightening speed, he stood slowly, his blood-soaked clothing feeling cold on his skin from the gust of air that blew through the gash in the wall.

He didn't know if she would make it, but if she didn't he determined that he would make her death count.

CHAPTER 11

Guillermo again found himself at the hospital, but this time as a visitor. They had managed to stabilize Dervish, but the doctors informed him that she would be in no condition to leave for a few days. He stood outside her door, his shirt stiff with her florescent blood, and he stared at the data chip in the palm of his mechanical hand.

What was on it?

Apparently she had wrested it from their invisible attacker, but his mind reeled with who that attacker might be. Whoever it was they were strong, and could take Dervish in a fight. It had also been invisible, a technology he was not aware was possible.

"I should fire you," said a familiar voice. "But then the Queen would only re-instate you."

Guillermo turned to see chief examiner Victor approaching, his hand resting on his holstered pistol.

"You nervous, sphincter?" Guillermo chuckled, slipping the data chip into his pocket. "You ought to know you have nothing to fear from me."

"You entered an unauthorized area, ordered one of the Queen's guards to help you commit a crime, and I am perplexed as to why."

"I left some embarrassing holos of me and your mom

in McFly's place and wanted to retrieve them."

Victor, surprisingly quick, pressed Guillermo to the wall with his forearm.

"Don't get in our way, Guillermo," Victor spat. "I may have to let you stay on the security force, but I don't have to let you stay here. You are being transferred to the City of Knowledge. You can live out your days pushing files around for all I care. Then you'll finally be useful to this organization."

Guillermo gripped Victor's wrist with his metal hand, hearing a slight cracking sound as the bug clicked his mandibles together in pain.

"I'm not going anywhere," he whispered, pulling Victor's hand away from him, the servos whining. "Not until I figure out who killed McFly and why. If you put your hands on me again, I'll do to you what I did to carrion gnats as a kid...pull their legs off."

Victor pulled away then and Guillermo let him go. He watched the chief examiner walk down the oval hallway, then turn around to face him once more.

"Expect the transfer today," he clicked. "Don't be late reporting for duty or even the Queen may not be able to save your job."

Guillermo wanted to fire off the last word, but Victor wouldn't have registered it because the chief examiner had already disappeared around the corner. Instead Guillermo kicked a nearby stool that tipped over and rolled into the hallway. When he turned around he saw one of Dervish's doctors quietly waiting for him to finish his tantrum.

The doctor was motioning for him to follow, and so he did, through the irising door of Dervish's room and to her bedside where she was finally awake, her hand motioning him to her in a strangely graceful manner.

"Guillermo," she croaked. "Please. I must speak to you."

He placed a hand on her arm and gently lowered it to her bed, staring at her with steely eyes.

"You have to rest, Dervish," he said. "Don't worry about me. I'll be fine."

She communicated to the doctor then, and he left the room displaying the irritated head waggle so common to his species. When he had left and they were alone in the room, she took his hand in hers.

"No," she chittered. "I must speak to you about the attack. Your life is in terrible danger. I am sworn to protect you regardless of outcome. Please."

"What is it?" he asked. "I'll be fine. You don't have to off yourself anytime soon."

"The chip. Do you have it?"

"Why?"

"When I...entered the apartment," she said, tilting her head back as a wave of pain shot through her. "The attacker was holding that chip in its hand, but it was...it smelled Terran..."

"No way, Dervish," he said, his fingers reaching into his pocket. "That thing was strong, fast. Couldn't be Terran...and it was invisible. Nothing has that kind of tech."

"It was Terran," she said, squirming in her bed.

"Terran... female...black armor."

Guillermo listened to her click away at the word, repeating it again and again: *Terran*. He sat in a chair near her bed, sinking down into it, the entire weight of his body melting, collapsing. But it couldn't be. They were all dead. He was the last one. He had been assured of it. His mind drifted away then, the doubt and confusion surrounding him on all sides. In his self-induced stupor Guillermo managed to rise out of the fog to begin thinking about the chip and what possibly could be on it.

As Dervish slipped away, her doctor rushing in to adjust her medication, Guillermo fumbled around in his pocket, his fingers searching for the chip. His eyes widened and his mouth stood agape as he found his pocket to be completely empty.

CHAPTER 12

"He lifted the crulling chip!" Guillermo screamed, his fists waving in front of him.

Dervish's doctor happened in just then but had to step aside as Guillermo bolted past him and sprinted down the hallway toward the nearest exit, his eyes scanning everywhere in search of Victor. He was met with blank stares, and when he rounded a corner a medical tech dropped a tray full of metal instruments which clanged and tinkled on the floor. Reasoning that the most possible path that Victor would take would be the nearest parking hangar, he weaved around hospital personnel, nearly knocking some of them down, a wrecking crew of speed and purpose.

Finally he reached the parking hangar where several rows of hover vehicles sat in neat lines, and far at the end of one of those lines a security force squad car was speeding away. Guillermo was sure that Victor was aboard. Fortunately Guillermo had parked his hover bike only a few meters away and he raced over to straightaway straddle it, fire up the engine and bolt out of the parking hangar nearly knocking an innocent visitor into a nearby parked car.

Traffic was murder.

Thick swarms of vehicles hummed and buzzed around him as he overrode the piloting software with a couple of angry strings of profanity and then weaved and bobbed around, over and under any vehicle not fast enough to prevent being an obstacle. He could just see Victor's squad vehicle ahead of him, jetting along at a leisurely pace, obviously not aware that he was being followed.

He sputtered out the words "security headquarters" and after a couple of seconds of clicks and whirrs he heard the familiar voice of Nancy over the comm.

"Can I help you, Officer March?"

"Hey yeah!" he shouted over the rushing wind. "Could you give me a location for the chief examiner? He accidentally left something with me that I think he'll need for the investigation."

There was a pause as he flew under a particularly slow delivery transport, his chest pressing close to the bike to miss one of the vehicle's lower, disc shaped repulsers. Guillermo thought for a second that he had lost the connection.

"I could get in touch with him…and I hear you are being promoted to inspector at the City of Knowledge station. Congratu —"

"Look, Nancy," Guillermo said, trying to keep his voice even so as not to register his angry tone with the hieroglyphic translator. "I need to speak with the chief examiner personally and I need to do that now. You read?"

"Affirmative," she said. "He appears to be landing at station headquarters right now, but he'll have to make it through the protestors. They aren't happy with the way the bombing investigation is proceeding. You want me to leave a message or have him wait?"

"Tell him to wait, but don't tell him it's me."

"Why not?"

"Just do it. I can't explain."

"I have to have —"

And Guillermo switched off.

He could see the station just ahead, a spherical black building with various blinking vertical antennae jutting skyward from geodesic tiles of silver grey. He dropped back on the throttle when he saw the massive crowd of bugs standing en masse, swarming near the entrance, their protest signs raised in defiance, anomilously silent to Terran ears but giving off a pheromonal cloud of angry demands. Victor's squad car landed just the other side of the mob, and Guillermo could see him climbing out of the vehicle, approaching the main doors as if he were going to the market to buy food for an evening meal. Guillermo gritted his teeth, slamming the bike into a hard descent, and landed directly between Victor and the roaring crowd, bouncing the bike's rear emitter on the pavement.

Victor drew his plasma pistol and trained it on Guillermo, as did several other nearby officers, and in seconds several of the mob began to turn, their focus now falling on the ensuing argument.

"Give me the chip, sphincter!" growled Guillermo, his mechanical hand flexing sporadically, the fingers twitching. He revved the bike's engine and the sound of it shook the ground.

Victor, sensing something from the crowd, put up a hand and the other officers lowered their weapons but kept them drawn.

"You had no right to keep that chip, Guillermo," said Victor matter-of-factly. "It is state's evidence and I could have you dismissed for stealing it."

"So let's look at it together, then. I have every right to —"

"Your rights are not in question, Guillermo. You are simply not…officially…assigned to this investigation. You need to report to the City of Knowledge as ordered. You are being promoted. You should be happy with your species' final service to our planet. Those files cannot wait."

Guillermo stepped off of the bike but left the engine running.

"What are you hiding?" said Guillermo, briefly turning toward the crowd who were now beginning to surround them. "What's on that chip that you don't want me to see? What are you covering up?"

The crowd began to press in and the security forces around Guillermo shook their heads in agitation. Victor stood his ground, his big compound eyes reflecting his surroundings like pools of black oil.

"I think you are traumatized from your ordeal these past few weeks," said Victor finally. "Perhaps you should take a rest once you reach the City of Knowledge."

Guillermo took two steps forward, and the security force raised their weapons, training them again on the Terran. He only looked at them and smiled, looked back at his bike, then glared at Victor. The crowd began to click and shake their crude signs.

"I'm going to take that chip from you now," Guillermo said coldly. "Now give it over or I'll rub your bug face in the pavement."

A silent signal was given, something Guillermo could not smell, but then the security officers were moving in, three of them reaching for electro-rods attached to their belts. He raised his fists and kicked backward at his bike, connecting with the throttle stud, sending the bike into a wild spin that caused it to slam into three of the security officers. Guillermo sprinted forward and tackled Victor to the hard pavement. Victor croaked as Guillermo quickly shot in with his mechanical fist and connected with the soft breathing membrane of the chief examiner's abdomen. Guillermo straddled him and began digging through the inspector's sleeve pockets for the chip, only to be knocked to the ground by an electro-rod.

The crowd became a frenzy of motion, several of the bug protestors moving in to stand between the security officers and Guillermo, but they fell limp when the officers strategically used their electro-rods in defense. Guillermo righted himself, kicking out at his attacker's knee and rolling to the left as the officer fell to the ground hissing. Guillermo leapt up, his neck and right shoulder tingling from the electro-rod, and he saw Victor trying to stand, his little clawed hand going for his left sleeve. Guillermo moved, grabbing Victor's arm in the iron grip of his mechanical hand and ignored the bug's squeal as he dug in the pocket to retrieve the small data chip.

As he was fumbling for the chip, the chief examiner caught Guillermo across the jaw with a right hook, and Guillermo let go of him briefly, only to counter with his own metallic fist.

He saw a spray of fluorescent green blood as his metal arm emitted a vibrating whine and began pounding Victor's chest again and again, the speed of the blows increasing in intensity and strength until his entire body vibrated with the attack. He tried to stop, but the arm moved independently, knocking Victor to the ground unconscious, and only then did it stop, leaving Guillermo with a searing pain in his back.

Guillermo screamed in disbelief at what he had done, how he had lost control. He shoved an innocent bystander away as he stumbled through the crowd, and then felt the sting of a plasma bolt as it tore through his right calf, causing him to stumble forward and fall on a passing protestor. The protestor, at first squirming, helped Guillermo to his feet and shielded him as another security officer tried to strike at him with an electro-rod. The rod struck his protector and Guillermo managed to stagger to his bike which had come to rest on its side a few meters away.

Another plasma blast crackled past his head. Wincing, he righted the bike and shot into the air, his arm now obeying his mental commands again. In the frenzied crowd below he could just see Victor standing to his feet, holding a glowing wound in his chest as he gesticulated orders to his subordinates.

The situation was rapidly spinning out of control.

As Guillermo shot back into traffic, weaving over and around the whirring hover vehicles, he saw that he had only been grazed by the plasma bolt, but it would need medical attention. He didn't have time to think about what the arm had done, but he wrote it off as adrenaline and thought faintly that it might be his emotions interfering with the nanite's connection to his nerve endings.

That didn't worry him as bad as the alert sirens that now grew louder behind him.

CHAPTER 13

Guillermo knew that he had to evade the security forces again, but this time he was not playing the role of the undercover cop. This time he had assaulted a fellow officer, had stolen crucial evidence, and had fled the scene pursued by several determined bugs in squad vehicles.

He had done it before, but not with an injured leg. He did, however, know exactly where to go. Earlier he had made a well placed call.

As he flew along, he leaned over to sneak a look at his leg only to find a burn mark obscuring the wound. The pain was bearable, so he thought that maybe he might only have been grazed. His arm was dripping with Victor's blood and he couldn't understand why he had lost control. His current situation was too overwhelming to think about what the arm had done, how it had acted on its own. His mind was also clouded with what Dervish said about the attacker in McFly's apartment being Terran.

That seemed impossible.

Choking down on the emitters, Guillermo was able to drop far below the traffic scanners and hover less than a meter above the lower level streets, blowing past startled bugs who either darted out of the way or stood silently by as he rumbled past them with his illuma-beams washing the gloom between skyscrapers in a soft blue light. Bits of trash and loose plasti-sheet scattered in his wake.

He had to ditch the bike as soon as he could, go on foot, as all vehicles on the planet were lo-jacked with hardwired traffic software. He found an alleyway, a dank place with rusted walls and heaps of trash piled here and there, used by vagrants and carrion wasps. Once he found a place to park he did some creative mechanical work, and after a few seconds he could hear the signature whine of a reactor overload that would cause a mini-meltdown, thereby erasing any trace of his DNA on the bike.

He really hated to ditch another ride like this.

As he finished up he could hear the distant call of security force sirens as they closed in on his position, their illuma-beams creating bright circles on the streets below. He had to move fast, and digging through a nearby pile of trash he found a scrap sheet of dura-plast, covered his head and shoulders with it, and limped off into the night. He tried to ignore the gut-heaving substance in which the dura-plast had been soaked.

He grabbed the communicator band from his wrist, admired the sleek design of its smooth metallic housing, then dropped it to the dampened pavement and crushed it under his boot heel.

"Never got to read the manual," he whispered.

He knew he had to get to the palace somehow, as he knew that there was no love lost between the Council of Eight who ran the security force. At this point he didn't feel like trusting anyone else. Dervish had been a stand-up girl. He hoped he wasn't throwing away his chances at freedom by attempting to contact Dlahuud.

He didn't know how he would contact her, but he somehow knew that it was urgent that he did.

He could smell the rotting vegetable odor of bug cuisine and knew he was nearing the back door of a solution. He hugged the wall and after glancing at the data chip, placed the shiny little disc in his front shirt pocket before reaching for his plasma pistol. Holding the gun out along the wall he pointed it at the door, his hand steady as stone. He heard a rattle of pans and a withered bug wearing a greasy apron stumbled out into the alley, a bucket of trash in hand. The old bug dumped it out near the doorway, accidentally covering the toe of Guillermo's boot.

"Great muttering J'Udaa, Gunny!" Guillermo growled. "Would you watch where you dump your trash?"

The elderly bug dropped the bucket, his hands reaching out to gently grab Guillermo's arm, the pistol reflected in his geodesic compound eyes.

"You plan to shoot me with that or shall I show you how to use it as a club?"

Guillermo lowered the pistol and shoved it into his concealed holster.

"Old man," he said. "I couldn't be too careful. Didn't know if you'd talk to me after that mess I made in your shop all those months ago."

Gunny made a vibrating noise with his mouth.

"I am grateful that I do not have to pay protection money anymore," he twittered. "Oh, you look like you took a hit...and what happened to your arm? Come on in and let me take a look at that plasma burn."

Guillermo didn't argue and only moved silently through the door behind Gunny as the bug led him by the hand like a small child. They walked past shelves full of hydroponically grown plants, and then cages with great purple gnats, big as a fist. Acceptable protein if properly prepared. They soon reached a store room that Guillermo found all too familiar.

"You wait here and I'll go get my kit," said Gunny, wiping his small hands on a filthy rag. "Drop your trousers…well, you know the routine."

"Sure," Guillermo said, but waited until Gunny had left the room to disrobe. He pulled the fabric gently away from the wound and heard the fabric make a slight crackling sound. With it came a new bolt of pain that ran up his leg and into his hip. It looked like he had suffered more than a graze, the skin around the open wound cauterized by the heat from the plasma blast. He stood with his pants down around his ankles, his finger poking around on the wound just as Gunny walked back into the room. The old bug dropped his medical kit on a nearby table with a clang.

"From the looks of you I would say you haven't washed your hands," Gunny said. "You could get a nasty infection. But I guess you know that."

"Yeah," said Guillermo straightening up and then leaning back against a table behind him. He flinched when his hand felt the slimy sensation of rotting vegetable matter that lay on top of it in neat little gooey piles.

"And do not touch the herbs," clicked Gunny. "All it needs is for some Terran to get his germs all over it."

Guillermo did not respond, only turning the wound on his leg toward Gunny as the bug produced a small tool with a spongy green blob on the end soaked in antiseptic. Before he could touch the wound with it, however, Gunny stopped, his mandibles clicking, silently staring at Guillermo's arm.

"Take a good look, then, Gunny," growled Guillermo.

"If you want I'll show you how crulling effective it is at pulverizing bug exoskeleton…and completely independent of my control."

Gunny didn't speak, only reached out with one hand and touched the metal elbow joint.

"Have not seen one of these models in a while. Looks like they spared no expense…and there are modifications."

"Modifications?" Guillermo said. "They didn't say anything about that. Said it was too expensive… something about a power source overload."

"Well, someone has made some modifications to the arm. If you look close there are some extra struts in there near the motor housing, something to give the arm more stability and power than normal. Could be bad if it rips out of your body. You mean you didn't know?"

"Not until about thirty minutes ago," Guillermo said, his voice low. "It just went crazy, started pounding away on my boss's face."

"So you are saying you are out of a job? You owe me money, Guillermo."

"Whatever, Gunny. I always owe you something. Just fix my leg so I can get on with being a legendary pain in sphinter's — "

Gunny held a slender hand up as he bent to examine the wound, his mandibles clicking randomly.

"Amazing," said Gunny as he placed the swab back in his tool kit and closed the lid. "I do not need to heal you. The nanites in your bloodstream are doing a fantastic job of knitting you back together. Part of the benefit of this particular brand of cybernetics...You mean they did not tell you about what the nanites can do?"

Guillermo touched his wound again, this time with his mechanical fingers, and noticed that the pain had indeed subsided. His stomach audibly told him that he was very hungry as well.

"Chert," he mumbled. "That's...something else they neglected to mention. Why didn't they tell me about this?"

"Did they at least tell you about the side effects?" asked Gunny.

"Not really," said Guillermo, reaching down to pull up his pants.

"Well," said Gunny, his voice taking on a resonant tone. "There were cases where the nanites went off of their programmed script and started to...modify...the subjects a little too aggressively. This all happened back during the occupation, so most of our race have forgotten about the horrors of that time."

"You mean I'm going to get modified? What do you mean, like a freak or something? Please tell me I'm not going to have an extra arm growing from my bum."

"Calm down, my friend," Gunny said, one hand resting on Guillermo's shoulder. "I think we can probably reset them...the nanites that is...if that begins to happen. It is possible the extra support rods were a modification that the nanites decided that you should have. The little machines are designed for war originally, you know. All you have to do to reset them is, theoretically, give the nanites a shock from a fusion power source. That should do the trick…or the process could kill you. No one has ever succeeded at this. It was designed as a form of control. Time of war and all."

"Then why did they give me this arm if they knew the probable outcome?" Guillermo said, wrapping himself tighter in the dura-plast, trying to keep his voice down.

"Perhaps they worked out the defects…or just didn't care," said Gunny with a shrug. "At least I hope so for your sake. If the arm becomes too powerful it will rip itself right out of you. The nanites are using materials found in your own body to repair your wounds, so you will need to eat regularly or they might start using material from other parts of your body they deem unnecessary. You might also think about the fact that the Phaedran Empire used to be able to track beings using the nanites, as they give off a power signature not easily masked."

Guillermo grinned, then grabbed a nearby bag of dried meat chips and began snarfing them down.

"That's why I came to you, Gunny," he said, his mouth full. "You have to take care of this for me. Not only that, I have this data chip I need to get into. Probably encrypted knowing McFly. You going to help me? As always I'll have to owe you."

"Certainly, Guillermo," Gunny said, his body language displaying frustration. "I will do what I can. Would you like some more food to take with you? The nanites will eat up any protein you do not need to survive. You are eating for several million now."

"Yeah, that's real funny," Guillermo laughed, forcing a

dry swallow. "Just get me out of here."

Guillermo pulled at the hem of his tattered, blood soaked shirt.

"And you have any threads I can borrow?" he asked. "Something preferably not covered in bug blood?"

Gunny nodded and left him then, and Guillermo stood for a few moments in the storeroom with the dura-plast wrapped around his head and shoulders, the creeping feeling that he had been betrayed always in the back of his mind. He tried to force that thought away, relying on his long relationship with Gunny who ran this restaurant as a front for his son's Terran tech smuggling operation.

Gunny's son dealt in contraband he hoarded from the Ontoccan Hegemony, the central government that kept all the other Five Rim worlds in line. The Ontoccans had made a fortune farming out the old Terran tech that had been modified and hybridized over the hundred or so years since the rebellion. Gunny's son, whom Guillermo called "Junior", had been running this illegal black market tech business for years, probably ever since he could carry a side arm. He had worked his way up in the Ontoccan tech industry and had been using his connections to make huge illegal profits. He was always on the look-out for new tech to modify and sell, and the bigger the tech the better. The Ontoccans had not caught on to his little operation as of yet, and both Gunny and Junior had gone to great lengths to ensure its secrecy.

Guillermo had always relied on old Gunny to patch him up when he was injured, hide him out when he was on the run or supply him with some new device Junior had crafted in the secret basement below their cold-storage lockers.

Favor for a favor, but bugs took life debts pretty seriously.

In a few minutes Gunny tottered back into the storeroom with a bundle of black cloth folded neatly in his arms.

"Got just the trick for you to lay low," he said, the monotone Terran speech taking on what Guillermo perceived as and excited tone. He tossed a bundle of clothing at Guillermo.

"This should suffice," said Gunny. "It is not high fashion, but it is functional."

Guillermo hastily changed into the loose fitting shirt and military style pants, having to tighten the belt a bit to accommodate the wider waistband.

"Could you have found pants that fit me? What kind of scrounger are you, Gunny?"

"It is all I could find at such short notice. Your race is gone, my friend. For this I am sorry."

"Yeah, yeah," said Guillermo as he fastened the magnetic clasps on the belt. "Hey, have you ever heard of an invisibility cloak or something like that? I mean, can you make someone invisible?"

The old bug placed a clawed hand on the back of his head and looked up at the overhead illuma-bulbs.

"Cannot say that I have. Why? Have you seen something like that? I could make enough to retire if I could get my hands on that kind of thing."

"Something attacked me in my old partner's apartment yesterday. Something tough. We couldn't see it at all until this brave girl struck it with her electro-glaive and even then it was just a shadow."

"Brave girl?" asked Gunny.

"Don't ask," Guillermo chuckled. "Queen's idea. She's like a bodyguard or something, but she's growing on me."

"A high honor. Looks like you are shedding your caste."

"No," Guillermo said. "Nothing like that."

Gunny made a hissing sound that Guillermo knew was a sign of amusement and ridicule.

"Since when do you need a babysitter?" Gunny chuckled.

Guillermo only squinted at him.

"However," Gunny continued. "I know that the Ontoccans have been working on a prototype but have not reached much further than the initial stages. It is very difficult to change the laws of physics, my friend. One cannot simply make something invisible, not completely anyway. And I will see what I can do about the chip. Should not be too hard to see what is on it. We will have to do that later, though."

A red light flashed on and off directly overhead where the ceiling met the wall, a little dome-shaped bulb that silently warned of impending doom. Guillermo had seen it before.

Security forces were near.

"Quickly," Gunny clicked. "Come with me. We shall

help you escape in the usual manner, but this time I will send my son with you and he will make sure you safely evade them."

"Unlike last time," Guillermo smiled. "Nearly didn't get away."

A shorter bug with several rebellious hieroglyphic etchings along his arms appeared in the doorway, most likely called by Gunny in his silent manner. Gunny reached under a table to his left, waved his hand, and the table sank into the floor revealing a set of stairs leading down to a cramped lift tube. He tossed Guillermo a small brown satchel and the contents briefly clanked and rattled.

"There are some things in here you might need. Also, my son has instructions to take you to the safe house. He will stay with you until I can join you. Is there anyone I might contact whom you trust?"

"Dervish," Guillermo said. "But she's in the hospital. I don't know how long she'll need to stay there. She was pretty banged up."

"I will do what I can as always," said Gunny. "Please. Go quickly. My son is very capable, and I will feign ignorance as always."

"Thanks, Gunny," Guillermo said. "I owe you."

Gunny swirled his hand in the air.

"You always will, but I will not forget what you did for me."

Junior was in the lift before Guillermo, but the Terran popped Gunny an old style salute before he backed into the small hallway, the table rising back into place to

throw them into complete darkness. As Guillermo felt
along the wall and entered the lift tube he heard the doors
whoosh shut and they began to plummet downward
toward the network of tunnels beneath the street.

The lower streets of Royal City were a crime infested
den of sudden and unexpected violence with dark corners
that even the brave dared not enter, but the catacombs
beneath the city were much worse.

CHAPTER 14

When the doors to the lift tube opened Guillermo and
the young bug were swallowed by the cold throat of
enveloping shadow that was the Undercity. Junior's
illuma-rod popped to life and Guillermo glimpsed
something slither away into the black hallway just at the
edge of the beam.

"I hate this crulling place," he murmured, and then
Junior handed him an illuma-rod of his own which he
happily activated and then drew his plasma pistol,
listening to the high pitched whine as it warmed up.

He had never heard Junior speak Terran, and as
young as the bug was Guillermo surmised that Junior
was one of the bugs who had never learned it. If Junior
couldn't speak Terran, then this trip to the Undercity
would be very interesting indeed.

Junior touched Guillermo on the forearm, making
him flinch. The young bug motioned for him to follow as

they shuffled down the dank corridor to an intersection, turned left, then along a tunnel that smelled of something old, something that had been rotting down here for a long time. A lichenous crust grew along the wall, and as the light from their illuma-rods washed over the growth, little spindly urchins flicked their spines, retreating into rusty metallic pock marks along the surface.

They continued on until they reached a vast cavernous area where glittered various pools of light, and as the objects in these pools took shape Guillermo saw the lowest caste of the bug race, the grey beggars, the outcasts, descendants of genetically engineered miners that built these tunnels long ago, driven mad by Terran forced labor and then forced to live down here as outcasts. From the nearest pool of light the squatty, thick-legged beggars scurried toward them, their humongous, clawed hands in front of them open with palms up, silently begging for any scrap of food or shiny object that they could scavenge. They scurried just as promptly back to their shabbily constructed huts when Guillermo pointed his pistol in their direction. The resumed their ritual of rutting around in the piles of garbage they had collected over the decades.

Guillermo scared them away absently, his eyes scanning the darkness for the shambling shape he saw when he first opened the lift earlier. Being on the menu was the more dangerous hazard.

They navigated along the path through the cavern that ran around and through the little glowing oases. The other grays understood, communicated by their brethren on other trash heaps that this Terran did not have anything to offer them but death. On the other side of the ominous room Junior led him to another tunnel leading down a steep grade to a network of twisting caves. This path eventually led them to a twenty-meter wide dome-shaped room faintly lit by illuma-orbs embedded in the ceiling high above. Several doors were equidistantly spaced about the walls, some of them embedded meters above the floor.

Junior beckoned him forward, and then stood in front of one of the rust and lichen covered black-metal doors. He produced a small oval-shaped device from a pouch on his sleeve and waved it around in a specific pattern before the door as if divining for water. The door opened, irising agape like a flower and shedding some of the lichens to the floor with a barely audible squeal.

A bright light came on inside and a long shaft of light shot out from the door across the uneven rock beneath his feet, illuminating the front of his body with a cool blue glow.

"In there?" asked Guillermo.

Junior only motioned for him to go inside with one outstretched hand just before he clasped it to his breast. A plasma bolt shot through him and then left a burn mark on the stone wall beyond. Guillermo spun around to see a band of three cloaked figures, their long-barrel plasma rifles trained on him, their bug mandibles barely visible beneath billowing black hoods. He didn't think, his adrenaline pumping, raising his pistol to fire off three consecutive shots at the attackers. He was only able to strike one of them, and the assassin slumped to the floor with a croak.

He darted lithely to his left, crouching down to make himself less of a target as the other two fired at him, one of the bolts striking his mechanical arm with a twang. He could feel the energy of the plasma bolt ripple down his arm and exit from his fingertips, a weird sensation that caused his stomach to churn. He fought this and fired back, the plasma bolt burning a hole through the neck of one of them and dropping him to the floor as if he were a stringless marionette.

Guillermo moved toward Junior who lay on the floor, the young bug stirring almost imperceptibly, and then ducked as one of the attacker's plasma bolts shot past him. The energy crackled millimeters from his skin so that he could feel the deadly electric heat of it. He fired back, the bolt searing the right hip joint of one of the remaining attackers. The assailant fell to the floor hissing, his rifle clattering across the black stone. The final attacker moved in, switching his rifle to auto with a nudge from his finger. A gout of plasma bolts erupted from the gun, ripping across the wall and threatening Guillermo. Guillermo braced for the worst, but just as the bolts came within centimeters of his head they climbed upward, cutting out as Guillermo squinted his eyes to see the shape of a silent predator crunching the hapless assassin in its massive jaws.

The thing in the dark had found them at last.

Guillermo scrambled, grabbing Junior and throwing him into the room. He turned his eyes on the ochre beast.

It was moving forward silently as if it sucked the sound out of the air, its eyeless oblong head a giant clam filled with rows of sharp teeth, its tail whipping back and forth tipped with a barb which slung acidic poison onto the floor with an acrid hiss.

He fired his pistol at it, the bolt striking the rough surface of its skin, but it moved forward unscathed.

He could hear a deep gurgle as he backed into the room. He activated the door behind him, stirring the air as it whooshed shut. A millisecond later the thing bounced against the metal door outside just as he secured the magnetic lock. He hoped that the plates would hold and scanned the dim room for an exit.

Opulent and well stocked with equal numbers of crates of food stuffs and illegal weapons, the room had only one exit: the door they just entered. He heard another thump on the door but tried to ignore it, thinking that the thing couldn't possibly get through the thick durasteel plate…

…but then again…

He examined the wound on Junior's abdomen. The plasma bolt had left a cauterized hole as wide as two of Guillermo's fingers. He could hear the boy's breathing, a dry wheezing sound from his damaged abdominal plate, but he thought that maybe Junior might survive. Perhaps one of the crates…

Thump.

He jumped, looked back at the door, then he cleared his throat and stalked toward the crates. He opened one of them to find five elongated slender rifles within, each of them nestled in a perfectly designed clasp that held them in place. Surely they had some kind of medical kit here in this safe room. He couldn't let Junior die.

Thump.

Faint lines of powder fell from the ceiling in various places, the dust visible in the recessed lighting along the walls. Junior rolled over, one set of mandibles clicking, tried to sit up, then immediately fell to the floor convulsing. Guillermo ran to him, pulling the small crates of foodstuffs away from the boy so that he would not injure himself further.

Thump.

He could see the middle of the oval door begin to buckle inward, the three plates that irised open beginning to separate. The magnetic lock must have partially malfunctioned. It hadn't completely failed or the door would blossom inward with the force of the creature's blows. Silence fell on him for a moment as Junior finished convulsing and lay still, so Guillermo grabbed him by the arms and dragged him across the floor and around behind the crates. He reached in and pulled one of the slender rifles from the one he had opened.

Thump.

This time, the door blew open like weakened flower pedals, the monster's tentacled feet slithering back outside, its jagged mouth agape as it tried to figure out how it would force its bulk through the small opening. It began to ram its clam-shaped head against the doorway, small bits of dust falling from the ceiling with each crushing assault. The mass of black tentacles it used for locomotion writhed and shot inside and then it tried to squeeze its bulk through the opening without success.

Guillermo caught himself staring, shook his head as if staving off sleep, then braced the rifle against his shoulder squeezing the trigger a little too hard.

Nothing happened.

"Chert," he muttered, holding the stock of the gun closer to his eyes. Something was missing from the gun. Across the room near the door, near the thing that wanted to eat him, sat a neat box with "ammunition" plainly labeled in heiroglyphs.

He hoped it was for this big gun he held.

Holding the rifle out in front of him as if its unloaded husk could do anything at all, he scooted along the wall. His back blocked one recessed light at a time until he neared the box. That was when the beast slammed into the door again, sending chunks of plasti-crete into the room. Big jagged blocks of it tumbled forward and the ochre beast fell clumsily into the room and onto its side, multiple tentacles wriggling, its deadly tail seeking a target.

As Guillermo reached for the box of cylindrical capsules, he wondered if they were indeed the ammunition he needed for this unknown rifle. He decided to chance it. Absently he noticed a black boot lodged between two of the beast's serrated teeth.

It roared at him then, a high pitched squeal combined with a deeply guttural roar. Expressionless, Guillermo grabbed one of the cylinders, a black liquid sloshing around inside it, and tried to pop it into the empty slot on the rifle. He fumbled around with his mechanical fingers and then dropped it just as the beast began to writhe toward him, knocking large and small crates aside with ease.

He grabbed another cylinder just as one tentacle shot out and shattered the box. Darting to his right, just narrowly missing the massive jaws that were now scraping ineffectively at the wall, he scurried backward, trying to slam the firing chamber home. Suddenly there was a satisfying whine of something inside of it warming up and spinning, what must be its firing chamber.

He pulled the trigger and something like molten metal shot out of the end of the barrel, forming meter long rods that flew through the body of the beast, embedding themselves in the wall beyond as it squealed in pain. He dove behind the crates, nearly landing on Junior who squirmed and chittered, but he could not tell if he was awake due to the expressionless state of Junior's insectoid face. Guillermo ducked as a tentacle shot out toward his head and he spied a smaller box lying only a few meters away.

"That'll help," Guillermo whispered.

The beast groaned, slapping away the boxes to get at the delicious Terran, angered by the pain of the cauterized holes that pierced its body but merely angered it. When the thing opened its jagged mouth and stuck out its grasping tongue, readying its barbed tail for a fateful strike, it caught something cube shaped and cold. It could feel the vibration in the floor of something skittering away to its left.

The beast wailed in pain as the box of grenades Guillermo had shoved in its maw began to erupt in a blast of deadly energy and flying shrapnel.

Guillermo lay on the floor just outside the door, covering his mouth with the collar of his shirt to filter out the smoke that was now billowing out of the flaming door. The remainder of the weapons coughed and popped in the blaze within, cooking the beast and filling the room with a foul odor like when meat is left on the grill too long. Junior began to stir beside him, raising one weak hand to shield his compound eyes from the glowing fire.

"Good thing I was here, huh?" said Guillermo raising up on his elbows and winking at Junior, checking his handy new rifle for damage. "Don't suppose you have another safe house. I kind of broke this one."

CHAPTER 15

Guillermo carried Junior, the young bug at first dragging his legs on the rocky floor but soon managing to pull one leg along to help. Guillermo didn't mind because Junior didn't weigh much, and he really owed the boy's father a heap of chids.

Junior had weakly shown Guillermo to one of the other doors across from the burning gun vault which turned out to be a secret passage leading into yet another network of tunnels and ancient mine shafts. Guillermo narrowly avoided the deep pits by squinting in the dim light of the fading illuma-rod in his hand.

"I want you to know that you owe me, kid," Guillermo whispered, just in case more of those beasts lurked in the unseen void. "Saving your backside from marauders and things from my nightmares should be a full time job, I guess."

Junior did not seem to understand Guillermo at all and only stared at him with his blank eyes, his mandibles clicking in a feeble response. Guillermo was glad the boy could at least respond, a sign that he was still alive.

Junior pointed ahead of them to a dimly lit opening on the other side of this maze of mine shafts. The light from the illuma-rod crept along the uneven black walls and hanging stalactites creating eerie shadows that slid by them like phantoms in the dark. They emerged into a larger room, its cavernous ceiling far beyond the reach of the illuma-rod's light. At the far end of the downward sloping cavern an ugly little blue glow bobbed and wavered, the light of a plasma-lantern. The light flickered as the sparks from the plasma warbled and flickered inside the lantern's transparent housing.

Guillermo extinguished his illuma-rod when he saw that there were figures standing around the lantern, their voices echoing up toward him with deep guttural growls and the soft familiar chittering of a bug's mimicry of Terran.

Even though his race was gone, this told him that two species were meeting, still using his common language to communicate.

Guillermo eased Junior down to the ground and then

crouched behind a giant lump of stone, reasoning that the distance from their new friends was enough that they would not be seen. Besides, if they had seen the illuma-rod before he deactivated it, Guillermo and Junior would probably already be on the run again.

"I hope these v'oshtus are friendly," he whispered, but Junior had drifted off to sleep. Guillermo hoped he wasn't dying.

He reached into the satchel and produced a pair of optics that fit directly on his face. Two lenses produced a nearly inaudible whir as they focused in on the meeting below him, and he started when he saw the ugly lower jaw of a Guajiin, its tusks jutting up nearly even with its fat bulbous nose.

Someone had set them at maximum magnification, so he touched a stud near one lens and the image zoomed out to reveal three Guajiin, one of them standing and the other two shuffling around in the darkness behind the first. Guillermo turned his head slightly and saw old Gunny standing in front of the one in the middle, his hands on his hips, which was a sign that he wasn't at all pleased and a little bit frightened.

Guajiin were intimidating even when in a good mood, their leathery skin scarred and tattooed by violent tribal rituals, their deep set black eyes, and four thick arms ending in massive hands. Mostly it was the half meter long revolvers they carried, weapons with which they settled all disputes. These weapons alone caused most beings to shudder.

Guillermo pulled a small ear-bud out of the right side

of the optics and plugged it into his ear, catching them in mid-conversation.

"...Terran bomb the low bad fortune," said the female Guajiin in the center, her long white hair in a braid at the base of her egg shaped skull. "I pay high pile Ontoccan clink to grasp much plasma shooters. You not renege? You spread much shame on clan."

"There is no need to fight," chittered Gunny. "I am your humble servant, Prutrath. Please understand that customs has been on high alert since the incident and we cannot risk moving them. If you will give me more time..."

One of the male Guajiin on her right side emerged into the flickering glow of the plasma-lantern, his face tattooed with a bright orange X, and Guillermo heard the deep vibrato of his laughter. It is never good when a Guajiin laughs. Usually it meant that something was about to have its arms pulled off.

Very slowly.

"No discuss more time," she said, her voice a deep rumble. "You do my word-will when mercs message back here. All you clan laid low today."

"Mercenaries?" Gunny said as he took one step backward. "You said nothing of this in the contract. No need for such drastic measures."

The third Guajiin stepped into view then, and Guillermo's teeth gritted together as he saw the familiar blue tattoos, the uneven tusks that jutted from the protruding lower jaw. He scanned down to see that one of the big male's hands were missing, a cauterized stump clearly visible.

"How the crull did he get out?" Guillermo growled. "I thought they jailed that dumb v'oshtu."

Just then Junior hissed loudly, holding his abdomen as he chittered out a quivering squeal of pain. Guillermo had turned away for a millisecond, but when he turned back the orange faced Guajiin and his old buddy from the sting operation were lumbering up toward his position. He thought briefly that he could fight, probably get a few rounds off before the two brutes could close in on him and grind him to paste, but he decided against it, and with a deep breath he exhaled out a few choice words in their direction as he stepped out from behind the rock.

The Guajiin did not stop, only dropping down to use all six of their appendages to race forward, their wide nostrils flaring as they lumbered toward him in the dark. The ogre-like monster didn't wince at all as he used his wounded arm to move him along somewhat awkwardly. Guillermo dashed sidelong, perpendicular to their advance, and fired off a few bolts from his new rifle. He muttered a curse as he struck the orange faced oaf in the face, dropping him to the stone floor, the burning rod impaling his head. The other, not phased, charged after Guillermo with haste.

He pulled the trigger again, but the gun fizzled, heating up in his hands, so he dropped it and ran.

"I scent you, betrayer!" he screamed, his voice a deep rumble. "I skin you! Scarf you whole!"

Guillermo ran along the wall as he tried very hard not to slip on the dampened floor. He fought looking behind him, instead focusing on the plasma lantern at the base of the cave where stood the female Guajiin, her giant pistol training on him. She was looking to line up a shot which would release a deadly piece of shrapnel as big as Guillermo's head.

He tried not to think about it, moving forward and down the steep hill, the Guajiin hot on his heels. He continued to run, hoping that Gunny would do what he wanted so that he could end the conflict quickly and easily. He couldn't communicate his plan to the old bug so he ran forward, getting closer to the plasma lantern.

That was when he fell forward on the rocky floor, his ankle in the iron grip of a massive hand.

He turned, twisting his body slightly to get a glimpse of his attacker, and noticed the familiar face of the Guajiin who had taken his arm.

"I mind-stored you face, Terran," he said as he hoisted Guillermo up by his foot and reached for his metal arm. "You would not snuff it high lofty. Take coward road to low pasture."

"I suppose you want to help me with that, then big fella?"

The stump, black blood now oozing from the end, jabbed at his stomach and took the wind from him. Guillermo grabbed the Guajiin's stump with his metal hand and thought about a vice.

His fingers bore down, servos straining, and carved a chunk of thick elephant skin from the Guajiin's already injured arm.

"Get some, Stumpy!" Guillermo shouted.

Guillermo was slammed to the hard floor just as he
was trying to get a breath, but lost all air from his lungs
and felt as if he had cracked a rib. The Guajiin relaxed
his grip a bit and Guillermo spun around, caught his
footing and gave the big brute a heavy metal uppercut.

"End Terran scamper!" screamed the female Guajiin.
"Bring him heart beating. You my yolk-slave, Gront!"

Guillermo spun in her direction, noticed that old
Gunny had backed far enough away, and watched as the
old guy fired directly into the whirling light of the plasma
lantern.

The explosion was deafening in the echoing expanse
of the cavern, and the female Guajiin was blown
backward, her unconscious body falling limply to the
floor. Guillermo was blown into Gront, but the Terran
had turned just so as to thrust his mechanical elbow into
the soft sternum of the big Guajiin, feeling the metal
creak in protest, his stomach feeling like he had been hit
with a hover bike.

Guillermo shook it off, sank to one knee, then stood
shakily and brushed off his shirt. He stooped down to
pull a communication band from the big Guajiin's wrist,
then pulled out his illuma-rod and lit it in time to see old
Gunny approaching him from the gloom.

"How did I do?" asked Gunny. "I was waiting until
you got clear of it before I fired, but you just wouldn't
move."

"Kind of busy, Gunny," Guillermo smirked holding
his stomach with one hand. "Thanks, though. But we
have more important problems. This Guajiin lady friend

of yours sent mercs after your son."

"Oh."

"He's pretty banged up," Guillermo said, motioning toward the entrance. "We have to get him to a med-facility soon or he might not make it. I'm really not sure."

Gunny pointed at the device in Guillermo's hand.

"What's that?"

"Comm band," Guillermo said. "Thought I could check on Dervish."

"I wouldn't advise it. I shouldn't have to tell you that the security force is probably monitoring every channel."

"I'm a big boy," Guillermo said. "Let's go get your son."

Guillermo led Gunny to the massive rock where Junior lay sleeping.

"I'll take him to The Skeev," Gunny said as he picked Junior up in his arms. "Follow me."

Guillermo took in a breath, his hand tightening on the comm band. Visiting The Skeev did not sound like a solution to any problem at all.

"Look Gunny," Guillermo said. "I think the idea of running was probably a good idea to begin with, but I really need to get to the bottom of McFly's murder. I think it's tied to the Council of Eight somehow…and there's another Terran. My bodyguard swore that it was a Terran that attacked us."

"But your people, Guillermo," Gunny said. "They're all gone."

Guillermo stared past Gunny, his eyes two steel orbs.

"I really have to get this data chip looked at. You said

you knew a guy?"

Gunny paused, his bottom mandible clicking like a metronome.

"I know a guy," he said. "But he works for The Skeev."

"Great," Guillermo said, letting out a sigh. "He and I...well..."

"I know," Gunny said. "You can count on my help."

They walked out the way Guillermo had come in, and they were long gone before Stumpy and his girlfriend woke up.

CHAPTER 16

Soon they were traveling a more familiar section of the Under City. He had hidden out here numerous times in the year he spent undercover, and the sights and smells of what was known as "Thieve's Sanctuary" assaulted his senses once again. Four races from all over the Five Rims congregated here, and the security forces dared not show their faces for fear of needing to call for immediate backup.

Everyone knew that The Skeev ran Thieve's Sanctuary.

Of course The Skeev was not a group but a brutal and rather monstrous Fraaz who was only mentioned in hushed tones, unknown to the city above.

This was by The Skeev's design.

"Do not make eye contact with anyone," said Gunny as they walked along. "Follow my lead as always."

"Yeah, yeah. I know the drill."

Just then a couple of bugs with ornate hieroglyphic designs carved into their exoskeletons approached them, long slender knives in each hand. When they saw Gunny and Guillermo carrying Junior they backed away. Several of the others clicked and chittered at each other, pushing the crowd aside for them as they shuffled down a darkened hallway lined with bugs who all had the same markings.

"My son is of their gang," said Gunny flatly. "The Iron Brood. They will take him to the surgeon and also see that we obtain audience with The Skeev."

Guillermo tried to pay attention to Gunny's words, but all he could think about was the unfriendly alliances he had made while hiding out down here so long ago. He hoped that those contacts were not around or, he hoped, had died. His eyes scanned the crowd constantly, looking for familiar faces.

Two of Junior's gang led them down a hallway opening into a greater room where two Aldrassans stood guard, their shiny ovoid heads and large black eyes reflecting the faces of those around them. They wore drab maroon tunics with jagged edges. These lean Aldrassans held staffs of carbonized flex-steel and stood on either side of a massive door. Guillermo knew that the Skeev's outer lair lay beyond this guard post.

One of the Aldrassans stepped forward flashing rows

of tiny sharp teeth that glistened in the dimly lit
antechamber.

"What business," he said, licking his thin black lips,
his six-fingered hands tightening on his staff.

"My son," Gunny said. "The Skeev owes me."

The Aldrassan sniffed the air and then sneered at
Guillermo.

"*It*...is not allowed," he growled.

Gunny wagged his head in disapproval.

"The Terran must come with me," Gunny protested.
"He is my traveling companion and therefore must pass
by my right."

Suddenly the Aldrassan's head cocked back as if he
were listening to something, and then with one swift
motion touched the round door behind him with wide-
spread fingers. The door irised open and the two
Aldrassans stood aside. Gunny and Guillermo carried
Junior into yet another darkened hallway.

When the door closed, Gunny stopped and faced
Guillermo.

"That was close," he said. "They really hate you."

"Probably my planet of origin, I would think."

Gunny clicked, then continued on, and the hallway
began to widen out and spiral downward along a steady
grade. The two of them moved along until they began to
hear strains of dark music, a thrumming of deep thumps
and melodic screeching. The hallway flashed with
tangerine and turquoise lights as they entered an
expansive room where several Fraaz hung from the
ceiling, their clawed feet gripping specially designed

rungs of what looked like shining brass. A few Aldrassan women, their sheer, skin tight clothing barely covering them, writhed in cages suspended from the floor by anti-gravity emitters. One of the Fraaz patrons reaching toward one of the girls with his leathery wing while she desperately tried to ignore him. One of these girls had proved useful in gathering some crucial intelligence about Death Adder last year, and he'd had to take the relationship too far.

She did not see him, and he was partially thankful.

The floor was crowded with dancing and mingling Aldrassans who had left Ontocca, eventually falling into crime in the Under City, their kind easily susceptible to a lurid lifestyle. The bugs in the room did not dance, unable to hear the music, but slowly swayed to the vibration they felt in the floor. Most of the bugs bore the same carved patterns on their arms as that of Junior, and when they saw Gunny and Guillermo carrying their comrade they crowded around the three of them, taking Junior in their arms and parting the crowd to make a path.

"Junior's pretty famous, I guess," Guillermo remarked.

"More like their leader," Gunny clicked. "My son has served The Skeev well, and it is because of him that you are not dead right now. My son's business is thriving."

Guillermo took this in stride.

"Did you mention to them that I saved his life? That's worth something, right?"

"Do not worry, Guillermo. The Iron Brood will take

care of my son, see to his care. If he dies many of the
leadership must end their lives as is their custom. Let us
see if we can find out what is on that chip of yours."

They shuffled through the crowd, moving ever toward
the back of the room where a long iridescent bar pulsed
with multi-colored lights. The patrons sitting at the row
of bar stools drank various concoctions produced by an
automated drone, a shining chrome orb with many
slender arms that filled glasses faster than any bartender
could.

Guillermo fell back a bit from Gunny, trying to make
it look like the crowd had separated them, and activated
the comm band, dialing Dervish's personal channel. He
waited, the familiar ring targeting his ear via a focused
beam of sound. She did not answer, and he wondered if
she was being held as an accessory until he heard a beep,
a signal for him to record a message.

Gunny turned around then, waving at him above the
crowd with arms flailing, and Guillermo finished his
message and put the comm band in a pouch on his thigh.
It was too big to wear on his wrist.

He joined Gunny, and as they neared the bar the air
pressure changed as one of the Fraaz detached from the
ceiling and swooped down in front of them, landing with
a thud. He rose up on all fours, his black fur bristling,
flashing his long sharp teeth at them and hissing loudly.
Guillermo prepared to force a fist into each massive
pointed ear, the Fraaz soft spot, but Gunny placed a
reassuring hand on Guillermo's shoulder.

"Terran filth," the Fraaz growled, his voice a

combination of screeching and deep rumbling. "It is only because of The Skeev that you live. Why have you brought this oppressor to our roost, armorer?"

"He has information," said Gunny. "And he saved my son's life. That is all you need to know. We have audience with The Skeev."

"The Skeev will not be pleased when he discovers that you broke the deal with Prutrath Nulaal, armorer. She was going to make us rich."

"She also sent mercenaries after my son, Tleen," Gunny hissed. "Common Guajiin tricks. I don't have time for your games, either."

Unseen by either Tleen or Guillermo, Gunny produced a tiny metal rod the size of a stylus and touched Tleen on his dish-shaped nose and a blue spark arced across the Fraaz's face. Tleen slumped to the floor and a faint odor of burning hair mingled with the scent of sweat and alcohol.

"Been meaning to test that thing out," Gunny said as he placed the stylus back in his sleeve pocket. "Mini stun-stick. Good for one use per hour, but it sure does make thugs like him think twice."

"Did you kill him?" came a raspy voice from a door beyond the bar.

"No Skeev," Gunny said patting the black fur on Tleen's head. "He'll wake up after a time with a huge headache."

A Fraaz, his fur bare on the left side of his body, bore pink scars from an incident long ago. Instead of the massive flaps of skin between long fingers common to most Fraaz, this wingless creature retained the long skinny arms that used to allow him to fly. Now he crept across the floor toward them on all fours, a ghastly grin across his toothy, mangled face.

The music suddenly stopped and all eyes were on the three of them.

The Skeev offered one clawed elbow toward the Terran.

"You must be Guillermo," said The Skeev. "Do we have business to discuss?"

"I think we do," Guillermo said, gripping The Skeev's clammy fingers. "That is if you are interested in solving my partner's murder."

"That is no matter, but come inside," said The Skeev, and they followed him into the pool of the black unknown beyond the bar.

CHAPTER 17

The Skeev crawled across the floor of his onyx dome-shaped office and Guillermo counted eight Aldrassan toughs moving aside to make a path as he and Gunny followed. A immense blood-red pillow lay on one side of the room, and The Skeev crawled awkwardly toward it, skirting a couple of oversized metallic chairs in his way. When he had settled in on the silken fabric, rolling around on his back so as to sink down and then raise his head to face his guests, he uttered a couple of high pitched barks in his native language which appeared to be some kind of command. The Aldrassans, wearing their drab maroon tunics, backed up against the rounded walls and held their carbon fiber staves in front of them.

Guillermo tried not to look at the curved knives they wore strapped to their skinny ankles, but he noticed nonetheless.

"Armorer," said The Skeev, indicating Gunny. "I have been informed that your son will make a full recovery. He simply needs to rest."

"Thank you, sir," Gunny said with a slight bow.

"Sit," The Skeev commanded. "I will call for a waiter to bring in a bottle of aavriil. Perhaps we can share it together, toast to peace before our business is concluded."

Guillermo sat in one of the hard metal chairs as did Gunny, a small red crystalline table separating the two of them. Guillermo rocked back in the chair briefly to test its weight.

"You have a data chip that is of interest, then?" asked The Skeev, settling into his pillow and grinning. "Perhaps you want us to decipher what is on it."

"I was told you had a techie who could access it," Guillermo said flatly. "I guess it just matters what you want in return for the service."

The scarred Fraaz produced a deep, wheezing chuckle, a gift from whomever gave him the ugliness makeover so long ago.

"Just like the Guillermo I remember. Cutting straight

to the matter at hand. Well, I suppose we can arrange for the chip to be deciphered. Simply hand it over and I will have my…techie…crack into it."

Guillermo shifted in his chair and then casually noticed one of the Aldrassans along the wall gripping his stave a little tighter. The Terran then spent a couple of seconds looking to his left, to his right, and then behind him where two of the Aldrassans stood in front of the door.

The only door.

"Forgive me, Skeev, but I need to be present with the techie," Guillermo said, his voice calm, almost monotone. "I need to go with the chip wherever it goes. It was my partners and I owe it to him to make sure it is handled properly."

Everyone in the room shifted a little except for Guillermo. The Aldrassans stood stoically, spaced evenly along the curved black walls.

"I assure you it will be in the safest and most careful of hands," The Skeev intoned, bearing his long sharp teeth briefly. "Are you not satisfied with my service from the last time we conducted business? I realize that we dealt with one another on a remote basis and not in person like today, but please do not insult my honor with this apparent display of mistrust."

"I *don't* trust you, Skeev," Guillermo said, stretching out his mechanical hand and then flexing the arm. "I don't trust anyone. That's why I'm still alive. That's how I survived that year of being undercover. Now I'd like to do business with you, but if you give me some chert about the tech's identity needing to be secret or some other nonsense, I'll walk. I don't work for the security force anymore and am pretty sure I'm fired. I'm also pretty sure one of the Queen's lackeys can crack this thing. I'm just seeing you 'cause you're close."

"Turn it over, Guillermo. Please." said Gunny, his hands in his lap.

The air in the room suddenly felt stale. Guillermo looked at Gunny, trying not to look incredulous.

"Whose side are you on, Gunny?" asked Guillermo, eyes narrowing. "Is this how it's going to be?"

The Aldrassans along the walls stood still, their staves in front of them, and The Skeev shifted on his pillow and grunted.

"Have you ever heard the story of the night of liberating blood?" asked The Skeev.

"Do I really give a chert?" Guillermo snapped, still staring at Gunny.

"It's a poignant story, I assure you," said The Skeev with a light laugh, a soft sound that would have been pleasing in another setting. In this humid room it sounded rather predatory.

The Skeev cleared his throat and continued.

"The Aldrassans had been oppressed by your kind for over two hundred years. Yet, they worshipped you as gods, building effigy after effigy, monolith after shining monolith in your honor, and in thanks for that your kind shipped them off to Ontocca along with the other races of the Five Rims to mine the world-mountain Coeus for precious ores. They are a passive people by nature, the

Aldrassans, and they spent a little over two centuries bowing before the Phaedran Empire. All the while the primitive Aldrassans formed priesthoods, performed animal sacrifices, and sold their children into slavery because that is what their gods required."

"Yeah, yeah. Terrans bad, Five Rims beings good," growled Guillermo, shifting forward in his chair and tensing his leg muscles. "I got your point, so now can we get on with the deciphering or should I just leave?"

He was watching the Aldrassans out of the corner of his eye, knowing the situation was falling apart by the second, that he wouldn't be leaving just yet. The Aldrassans along the wall began to move closer, their staves gripped tightly. With a wave of The Skeev's little clawed hand Gunny stood, his decrepit knees popping. The old guy backed away, slipping past the Aldrassans and out the door they had entered.

Guillermo hung his head, relaxed his arms.

"Sorry, Guillermo," said The Skeev. "My money is better than the old armorer's loyalty I suppose."

Guillermo cleared his throat as the door behind him irised shut again.

"I will continue," said The Skeev, his beady right eye closing, the other eye perpetually open due to the scarring. "One beautiful arid day in the middle of the summer, during the hundred year war of attrition that we mounted against your kind, a lone Aldrassan, a slave named Duruk, one day rebelled against his master. He pushed his elderly Terran master down the stairs after he could suffer no more abuse. The Terran's head burst open, and after hiding for days in an ancient catacomb, struggling with his faith, Duruk formulated an idea.

"The gods were not gods at all, he reasoned. They were mortal like any other being, and if they were mortal then they could be eradicated. The Aldrassans finally felt the same as all the other races in the Five Rims. It just took them longer.

"That night old Duruk developed a plan, and after sharing his new found knowledge with many of his kind, slit the throats of every Terran on Aldrassas in one night, the night of liberating blood. They slit their throats while they slept, the Terrans completely confident that these primitive Aldrassans did not have the means or the will to oppose them."

Guillermo tightened his fists, looked at The Skeev and began to laugh.

"That's a nice story, but it is a myth," said Guillermo. "Something Terran mothers used to tell their unruly children."

The Skeev leaned forward, propping himself up with his long wingless arms.

"The story doesn't end there," The Skeev said, his gnarled face twisting into a menacing toothy smile. "Duruk became the new god of Aldrassus for a short time, but during his reign the people of his world saw the brutality that had been taught to him by his overlords, and soon his own people rose up against him and killed him as well. The remainder of his personal guard of assassins were said to have fled Aldrassus, and now plot the death of Terrans wherever they roam."

"Well, that's nice," Guillermo sneered, his hand gently resting on the little crystalline table.

"In fact, you are surrounded by what is left of The Champions of Duruk right now," The Skeev said, his voice a low growl. "It took a considerable effort to get them here. And they think you should hand over the chip."

Guillermo glanced to his left and right, seeing the faces of the Aldrassans, their tiny needle sharp teeth bared, their giant black eyes reflecting his face.

"No chert," Guillermo said. "These are just a bunch of —"

Thwak!

One of the Aldrassans returned to the wall as swiftly as he had struck, his carbon fiber staff still vibrating with the blow he just landed, Guillermo's blood trailing across the floor.

"I suppose we can work something out," Guillermo offered, wiping the blood from his mouth with the back of his hand and then feeling around inside his mouth to remove a loosened tooth. "There's no need to let this get nasty."

"That's the spirit," The Skeev hissed. "Now just hand over the chip and we can make this quick."

Guillermo glanced over his shoulder and grinned at the Aldrassans standing guard at the door, then turned back to face the mangled face of The Skeev.

"I hope you made arrangements, Skeev," Guillermo rasped. "Because I'll die before I give this chip up."

Guillermo's metallic hand clamped tightly on the little

crystalline table and flung it at the Aldrassan who hit him. The Aldrassan blocked it with his staff, shattering it, sending tiny shards of red crystal shooting toward the now screaming Skeev, his long skinny arms trying desperately to shield his lumpy face. The Aldrassan shot forward, his staff at the ready, but with one motion, Guillermo stood and brought the full force of his fist upward like a rocket against the Aldrassan's jaw, knocking him to the floor.

Guillermo reached down and pulled the knife from the fallen Aldrassan's ankle sheath then side-stepped and grabbed Gunny's chair, flinging it at another guard who was twirling his staff. The Champion of Duruk easily batted it aside with his carbon fiber staff and snarled.

Guillermo's only chance was to make it to the door.

Before he could move further he was surrounded by three more Aldrassans, and from behind he felt the burning sting of one of the Champion's curved knife blades plunge deep into his lower back.

Guillermo groaned, but didn't lose his footing.

Couldn't lose his footing.

He raised his mechanical arm almost instinctively, a shower of sparks causing him to squint as the Aldrassan's staff slid down his forearm. His fist clenching the stolen knife. He crouched, spun on the ball of his foot, and slashed low behind him, severing a tendon just above the knee of the attacker who had stabbed him. The Champion did not let out a cry, answering this by striking downward with his staff, catching Guillermo's metallic shoulder joint. Guillermo shouted and then rocked backward, standing up into an Aldrassan behind him who was readying a blow. The crown of the Guillermo's head crushed the Aldrassan's weak jaw, and Guillermo saw bits of tiny sharp teeth fall like enamel rain. Guillermo spun again, knocking his opponent to his back and then he continued forward, leaping in the air to land one booted heel on the injured Aldrassan's neck.

There was a satisfying crunch, but he was outnumbered and he knew it.

The one he had uppercutted was waking up, and as he spun around, his back to the wall, The Skeev was producing a plasma pistol. Three more Aldrassans were leaving their place against the wall and stalking forward toward him.

He glanced at the door, noticing that the two Aldrassans had not left their post, just as another staff struck him across the cheekbone. He felt darkness wash over him for a second, but then he backed against the wall, his mechanical arm suddenly seeming to fail him.

It was frozen to his side.

They stalked toward him, but then he heard a whistle from The Skeev.

"Hold," said the Fraaz, trying to adjust his position on the pillow and hold the pistol with the five clawed toes of his foot. "Don't kill him. He is worth too much to her alive."

Guillermo looked at the door again, desperately trying to move his arm, but the arm was unresponsive.

How do I make this crulling thing work?!

"There is no use, Guillermo," said The Skeev, his

voice low and calm. "Your kind is a fossil someone finds in a stream. Terrans are nearly extinct, a long dead species who were dead even before they left their cursed solar system. They fed on the Five Rims like a withered blood-worm, using our resources before being removed like the parasite that they were."

"You watch your mouth, Fraaz," Guillermo said coldly, glancing at the door again. He held the knife in front of him, blade down. He had to stall for time.

"How about you and me settle this the old Terran way," Guillermo shouted, his voice shrill, blood dripping down his back. "Get down off that pillow, you old v'oshtu and show me wha—"

The Skeev burst forth on all fours, and with a loud snarl broke through his Champion guards and tackled Guillermo to the floor, pinning him down with his long skinny arms and twitching clawed hands. Guillermo screamed as The Skeev bit deep into the Terran's shoulder with long serrated teeth. Crimson blood sprayed across the drab maroon tunic of an Aldrassan whose thin lips parted in a glistening sneer.

Guillermo had fallen with his arm across his chest, the knife blade toward his enemy, and now with his other hand he drove it into the hard chest of The Skeev, but he did not penetrate the Fraaz's thick breastbone. He heard the blade grating on it as he desperately tried to force it home.

His arm wouldn't move.

"You cannot kill me, Terran," snarled The Skeev. "I will drink your blood just to the edge of your death and

then leave you for our benefactor. She has paid a fortune
to have you brought to her in chains."

Guillermo grunted, every ounce of his mind focused
on his arm. Why would it not move? What was wrong
with it? He screamed, listening to the laughter of the
Aldrassan Champions of Duruk. The Skeev's long
pointed tongue began to feel around in his shoulder
wound, lapping up the blood as it oozed out.

"Move!" Guillermo shouted to his useless arm, his
voice quivering. "Moooove!"

The Skeev paused, cocked his head back, Guillermo's
blood coating the Fraaz's long serrated teeth.

"I am The Skeev," he said. "I will move when it
pleases me to do so."

The Skeev continued drinking Guillermo's blood, and
he was beginning to feel cold. Something like tiny stars
began to circle the edges of his vision, and then he was
shaken by his arm suddenly coming to life.

In one smooth motion, he made a fist and brought it
up into the soft lower abdomen of The Skeev, hearing a
sickening crunch as the blade passed the bone and broke
off inside. The Fraazian rolled to his left, his final retort
an unintelligible death rattle as he slumped to the shiny
black floor. Guillermo scooted to the wall, his thighs
burning, and in his fading vision saw the Champions of
Duruk begin to close in on him, each of them twirling
their staves, making loud whooshing sounds that echoed
from the curved black walls.

Guillermo somehow managed a laugh, each breath
accentuating the stab wound in his back.

"We will avenge our savior," said one of them, his tiny sharp teeth biting into his lip and bringing forth blood. "With your death, our mission is complete."

"Bring it," Guillermo said, closing his eyes.

As he fell out of the light he felt a new pain strike him in the chest, then heard the whoosh of the door irising open. A draft of cool air drifted across his wounds, and in the haze he saw something spinning and heard the familiar vibrating swish of an electro-glaive.

CHAPTER 18

"Guillermo…"

"Guillermo…please…"

"Guillermo…you must awaken…I cannot do this alone…"

As his eyelids cracked open he felt a palpable dark, followed by a horrible stench and a feeling that he was sitting in a cold stream. Dervish was crouching over him, the energy from her electro-glaive sending a soft blue glow onto the jagged patterns decorating the walls and ceiling.

"We have eluded them for now," she said. "But we have to keep moving. I beg forgiveness for my inability to carry you any further. I am not fully recovered."

Guillermo sat up, the pain in his back a reminder of the knife wound from earlier. The ammonia in the air forced him to cough and his eyes burned.

"Great *Volsuun*," Guillermo gagged. "The sewer?"

He paused, grateful he wasn't dead at least.

"What now?" he asked. "How did you get me out of that room?"

"It was...difficult," she managed. "The Aldrassans followed us down here, but so far I have managed to elude them. However, the sewage is preventing me from sensing them by normal means, so I am in need of your assistance. What did they want of you?"

"The chip," he coughed. "McFly's chip. They were going to take it. Said someone was paying them a fortune to get it, to get me. Were going to give me over to someone. Someone who wanted me alive."

"Do you still have it?" she asked.

He fumbled around in his pocket and then groaned. He pulled out the chip which was now in two pieces.

Guillermo spat out a string of curses.

"It appears that now we need to get out of our current situation," she said. "I am sworn to ensure your safety."

"Yeah yeah. Ok. But really. Thanks."

"Your thanks is not necessary. Only your compliance. Can you move?"

Guillermo tried to sit up, but the knife wound in his back and the oozing sore where The Skeev bit him burned and throbbed. He fought through it and shakily stood to his feet, his hand moving along the slimy wall for balance.

"I guess I'm good to go," he said. "You lead the way."

He limped along behind her, his eyes slowly adjusting

to the gloom, his nose not capable of adjusting to the sickening odor of sewage. He tore some of the bottom of his shirt and wrapped it around his mouth and nose, but it was little use. His feet slipped now and then, but he managed to keep his balance by feeling along the grimy walls. The sewer tunnels were long tubes that gradually angled down toward various central hubs where they split into several other tubes which also angled down. He assumed that they would eventually lead to a water source or a gargantuan composting machine, some of them greater than most starships. He'd only read about them, of course.

After about an hour they emerged into one of the hubs and he began to see silver spots of light in the darkness, his brain slowly succumbing to the effects of the ammonia in the air. His lungs and nose burned and his bitter tongue rolled around in his mouth dryly.

"I have to get out of here!" he shouted, his lungs on fire. "I can't take much more…"

He fell, his knees splashing in the slimy ooze, splattering Dervish who spun and caught him just before he face-planted in the sickening flow.

"Just a little further," she said. "I will help you. The next hub will be a way out, I feel."

She put her head under his metal arm and he felt her take him as his legs became weak, the lines of reflected light along the walls fading away as the blood loss began to put him to sleep.

The hub was a colossal cylinder with many tunnels leading off in evenly spaced directions, a pool of sewage in the center, and a titanic tube above that dropped a steady stream of liquid down into the chamber.

"No place like home," he slurred, his eyelids drooping, a small smile fighting to emerge. "Is this the escape you told me about?"

Guillermo's eyes squeezed shut, delirious, and he shook his head to stay awake, but when he opened his eyes he saw three Aldrassans in one of the tunnels, their staves in both hands, knees bent in a posture of attack.

One of them charged silently forward.

Guillermo fell to the floor, splashing grimy sewage in every direction, and he rolled to his side to see Dervish sever the head of the Aldrassan with one swipe of her electro-glaive. The two others circled her, and she impaled another Aldrassan, ran up the wall using her embedded glaive for support, then down the other side to rip the glaive out of the wound as the second attacker fell to the floor.

Guillermo pushed up and out of the muck with every ounce of strength left, trying to make his legs work, but the only limb not completely fatigued was his mechanical arm. He pulled himself along, listening to the metal scrape the grit that lined the hard floor.

As Dervish spun to face the third attacker, a fourth emerged from another tunnel and charged her, but she did react, did not spin to face him like the others, and Guillermo knew that the sewage was preventing her from sensing him. He cried out, an unintelligible grunt of anguish, but the fourth attacker descended on her with a curved blade, plunging it into her back.

Guillermo pushed himself up, rocked back on his knees, and took in a deep breath, feeling the ammonia burn his lungs again, but this time it didn't burn so badly, and he could feel a surge of energy from somewhere deep within him. Before he could think another thought, he was standing, then running, his metallic fist straining the carbon fiber cords in his forearm. In seconds he was on them, pounding away at them with an abandon that resembled an animal, his eyes wide, his teeth clenched.

Dervish fell away, her hand reaching for the knife embedded in her flesh but not able to reach it. Guillermo was incensed, his heart thumping in his throat, his eyes two white orbs in the dark as he crushed bone and roared in anger, saliva spewing from his mouth. Soon the quiet creeped in like a soft breeze, the Aldrassans dead at his feet, and Guillermo stood silent, his shoulders rising and falling as he breathed the tainted air in loud gasps.

"Guillermo," Dervish clicked. "What happened to you?"

Guillermo turned, his teeth bared, his eyes a fire of rage, and he started toward Dervish just as a roaring torrent of fluid emptied into the hub and washed them down, down, down. They fell for what seemed ages, finally slowing as if gravity had lost its grip on them, only to plunge into the cold blackness of a peculiar underground lake.

They fought to the surface, every stroke a painful effort, and in the murky blackness they could just make out a rocky shoreline.

CHAPTER 19

"Where are we?" Guillermo asked, his chest rising and falling rapidly.

They lay on a rocky surface near water, but Guillermo only knew this from the sound of small waves he heard lapping against the shore. The darkness filled his vision as if he were blind, but at least the air in this place was less offensive. He caught a faint aroma of ammonia on the air, but it was not as intense as before, and the air was much cooler as if climate controlled.

Dervish had not responded.

"Hey," he grunted, propping himself up. He noticed that his wounds now itched terribly but remarkably the pain was gone.

"I am here," chittered Dervish. "It appears that the maker has spared us once more. How are your injuries? I am to your right. Touch me if you are awake."

He fumbled to his right and found her there.

"I assume you are in shock," she said, and he felt her clammy hand on his neck.

He flinched, and she pulled her hand back posthaste.

"Are you going to attack me?"

"No," he said, then pulled her hand close to his face and shook his head from side to side.

"I see," she said. "I am thankful that you spared me."

"It's not like that," Guillermo said, realizing he

couldn't be heard and then tightening his lips. No use talking to someone in the dark who can only read lips. Frankly, he didn't remember trying to attack Dervish, but did remember becoming extremely frustrated and angry. The thought faded away as Dervish continued.

"I must find a light source. I lost my weapon in the fall. Perhaps it is at the bottom of this lake."

He remained silent.

"My vision is slightly impaired, but this cavern is immense. It is something unknown to me. I was unaware that this place existed."

Guillermo felt around him, then stood to his feet. He had to adjust his balance a bit, but found Dervish in the dark and helped her up. His hand felt the knife still embedded in her back and she hissed.

"I probably need to get that," he said. "Do you think I should pull it out?"

"Pull it out if you can," she said. "Please remove the knife…carefully."

He felt for the knife again and with one swift motion pulled it from her flesh. She hissed again, and he felt her brace against him, the strength in her hands causing him to wince as they nearly crushed his arm.

"Easy there, Dervish," he said. "No need to replace my other arm just yet."

He felt her hand on top of his head, gently grasping at his hair.

"I will take your hand and lead you along the shoreline," she said. "Nod if you understand."

He nodded, and then she felt along his shoulder, down

his forearm and grasped his hand. Soon they were
gingerly creeping along, kicking along the ground for any
rocks that could trip them up. They rounded a massive
piece of wet stone that Guillermo assumed was a wall,
and beyond he could see faintly in the darkness a soft
flickering light, the ripples in the lake reflecting its orange
glow in wide curving half-circles.

The two of them hugged the wall as they moved, the
shoreline becoming more and more narrow, and as the
light grew brighter they noticed that it was emanating
from an illuma-bulb that was mounted far above the floor
of the cave. A zig-zagging staircase cut into the rock wall
lead up toward the light, and Dervish extended her arm
behind her to place her hand on Guillermo's chest. They
stopped and then she turned to him, her mouth clicking in
soft tones.

"The stair is ancient," she said, her black eyes two
large dots in the dim light. "As I said, it is not familiar to
me. Perhaps I should scout ahead and see what dangers
are present."

Guillermo placed a hand on her extended arm and
gently pressed it away from him.

"Where you go I go," he whispered. "We've come this
far. We face this together."

She nodded, and then moved to the stair, her posture
in a low crouch as she climbed the onyx black steps.
Guillermo followed, noticing that in the faint light it
seemed that the steps were not carved from rock but
made from the same chitinous substance of which all
traditional bug buildings consisted. They climbed higher

and higher, no sound save their light footfalls and the gentle lapping of the water against the shore below.

Soon even that faded.

As they approached the top, some two hundred meters from the shoreline, Guillermo had to squint his eyes and shield them with his hand. The big round orange orb was embedded in the wall above an oval metal door that looked like it belonged at the entrance to a vault. A short, thick metal handle protruded from the center, but Guillermo could not see a security panel or any other form of activation. The door, shining and new, seemed out of place in this ancient cavern.

Guillermo touched Dervish's shoulder and she turned to face him.

"Where are the guards?" he asked. "Don't you think they'd have guards, whoever they are? Or is this the back entrance to the palace?"

"I am not familiar with this door," she said. "And the door alone may be all the guard they need, whoever they are. I sense ozone, as if the door is charging the air around it. It is most definitely encased in an energy field. Do not touch it."

"I wasn't planning to."

They stood quietly staring at the door for a few moments, and then Dervish placed one hand on the rock wall on the left side of the door.

Nothing happened.

"Don't do stuff like that!" Guillermo whispered loudly. "That thing is probably trapped."

Dervish began staring at the door again, and

Guillermo paced for a second, shook his head, then with a deep sigh and a string of Guajiin profanity grabbed the thick metal handle with his metallic arm. Dervish threw her hands in the air and hissed as a painless crackle of energy rippled along his forearm.

"Hey, this isn't so bad," he said as he pulled on the handle, finding that it easily turned to the left. "Don't feel a thing. Guess it's the rubber coated fingers."

The door separated along a seam around the outside and then swung in. Guillermo released it and then they were staring down a long tunnel that had been carved in the rock.

Far beyond he heard something that sounded to him like evenly timed thunderclaps.

"You sense anything?" he asked.

She stood in the open doorway for a moment, then backed up and faced him.

"I cannot say," she said, her body language showing agitation. "It is our only way through, but it will be very dangerous. I sense many of my kind."

She froze, her top mandible opened and closed.

"Someone is coming."

"Yeah, I think opening this door was probably our first mistake."

They backed away, separating and leaning against the outside wall just as Guillermo reached above them with his metal arm and destroyed the orange luna-bulb. It shattered and rained small shards of plastic down on his head, some of it going inside his collar and scratching at his back.

"Chert!" he exclaimed.

Darkness.

They waited, the moisture in the cavern condensing and falling into a puddle somewhere, the soft sound of dripping water echoing somewhere in the darkness.

Two shapes exited to the small landing at the top of the stairs and Dervish was between them before they could react, her small hands jabbing at them, and before Guillermo could raise his fists to prepare a reaction the two guards were lying on the floor unconscious.

"Military caste," she said. "What are they doing down here?"

"And where is *here* exactly," Guillermo said, shifting one of the soldier's legs with the toe of his boot.

"We can only assume that we are moving in the right direction," she said. "However, if these soldiers are down here, then that means there is a way out. Our biggest problem is that they will sense you before they sense me."

"Yeah that's pretty obvious," said Guillermo, grabbing a plasma rifle from the floor and then stepping past the unconscious guards and Dervish and then into the tunnel. "But I don't see another choice."

CHAPTER 20

The tunnel descended at a slight angle and Guillermo had to keep Dervish within arms length so as not to be lost in the darkness, her footfalls nearly inaudible. They stumbled along, the air around them becoming thick and moist, as if they were descending into a giant sauna. The smell assaulted him first. A powerful, oily, industrial smell, and again the thunderclaps that echoed up the tunnel, thunderclaps that now sounded like the unified stomp of boots on a hard floor.

Dervish pressed a nimble hand into his chest.

"Three guards ahead," she said. "Military caste. Carrying plasma rifles."

She forced him against the wall with a strength that seemed greater than her stature was capable.

"Wait here. I shall eliminate them. I will return when I finish."

He grabbed at her but was only able to brush her with his fingertips.

"Wait," he said. "If we take out enough guards, don't you think they'll go on alert? I'm pretty sure these guys check in now and again."

"What do you wish for me to do?" she asked. "I am at your command, but I must insist on swift action. Your plasma gun will certainly alert them. My unarmed attacks will not."

Guillermo rolled this around in his head for a moment, then took in a sharp breath.

"There's no argument about how lethal your fists are, Dervish, but eventually you're going to need my gun. Let's stick together."

"I again advise against this, but if it is your wish I will do my best to keep you safe. I am sworn to protect you."

He only shrugged at her repetitive command protocol, then indicated their next action by pointing down the tunnel toward the light. She crept forward, slowly at first, but then she was moving at full tilt, and they reached a small round room where she made quick work of two more guards while Guillermo stood by, gun powering up with a high pitched whine. Guillermo's only contribution was raising his eyebrows and grinning slightly.

He stood within an enveloping shadow against the wall and peered out the doorway into a massive underground cavern. In the faint glow of an overhead light source far above, rows of interceptor class Terran war bikes sat moored in holding clamps, their armor edged in slight traces of rust. Several clusters of maintenance crew bugs stood around them, orange and yellow sparks shooting out in various directions as they worked to repair the ancient war machines.

More intimidating were the rows and rows of bug soldiers, thousands of them carrying plasma rifles, marching in drill formation toward a huge exit on the other side of the cavern.

Guillermo jumped as two bug guards shuffled by, their plasma rifles spinning up, and Dervish stood calmly by the door before turning in his direction.

"How are they not seeing us?" Guillermo mouthed. "Do they see us?"

"No," Dervish chittered softly. "I am masking our scent while mimicking the scent of these two guards I just disabled."

"Dervish your talents amaze me," Guillermo said. "Remind me to give you a raise."

"But you are not paying me, Guillermo," she clicked. "I do not understand."

"Never mind. You see a way out of this?"

She looked through the doorway, her hand resting against the round door frame, her lithe body just inside the dark archway. A few moments later she turned and came close to him, her clicking mandibles inches from his face.

"There are three hover bikes on the left hand side of this cavern beyond, not far from this door. I am certain that I can get you to one of the bikes, but we will have to recode it to one of us in order to activate it. I have not seen these vehicles before, only in history holos. They have been modified heavily."

Guillermo moved his thumb over the full auto activation stud on his rifle.

"You get me over there and I can crulling hot-wire anything."

She did not waste any more time, stepping out into the hangar bay calmly as if she belonged there. Guillermo followed, his hands gripping the stock of the rifle tightly. He was shaken out of his trance by sudden plasma bolts that baked the air next to his head. The bug soldiers, their green carapaces reflecting the orange light of the welding sparks, raced toward them in eerie silence, the only sound their plasma bolts and hurried footfalls on the echoing hangar bay floor.

Dervish dropped to the deck and with one sweep of

her leg tripped up one of the guards who strategically fell into another. She stopped for only a brief moment to strike them in that vulnerable spot of which she was so fond before ripping a chest plate off of one of them and moving on. Guillermo listened to his plasma rifle scream as he lay down a swath of blue-white crackling beams that left trails of glowing pale dust hanging in the air like tinsel. His plasma blasts struck a few of the soldiers, but then as he neared the bikes he saw that their emitters were fastened to the floor with mooring clamps.

"Chert!" he shouted, his boots skidding on the floor as he came to a stop.

Dervish fell in behind him, but before he could blink at her she dove in front of a plasma bolt and slumped to the floor at his feet, laying motionless. He turned and activated the trigger stud, his knuckles turning white on the gun as he fired into the mass of soldiers scurrying toward him, a horrified and desperate scream exploding from his throat. He did not have time to check Dervish, to see if she was dead, and as the soldiers moved closer and his power cell went dead he threw the gun at one of them, knocking the grunt to the floor.

Guillermo's metallic arm tensed up, but this did not register in his fevered brain. He moved fluidly about, and when plasma bolts struck him they ricocheted from the arm that now emanated a purple energy field. He mindlessly went to work on the soldiers until they backed away from him. Raging, his eyes wild, he swung at them like an animal.

"Officer March," came a chittering, high pitched voice

from the back of the crowd. "Stand down or you will not survive. My soldiers are nearly endless in supply."

Guillermo did not hear the voice, his teeth clenched, saliva dripping from his mouth. He screamed again, swinging at the crowd of soldiers who were now backing away from him.

Some of the soldiers parted ranks and out stepped the princess, her royal golden garb replaced with a green metallic battle suit, modified from old Terran tech. She held in her hand a small metallic orb which projected an interface that she manipulated with two wriggling fingers. Guillermo's arm became rigid then and his entire body froze in place.

"It appears that the control is being overridden by your force of will," she said, her head cocking to the side. "It would also appear that the nanites are being recoded by your brain waves, somehow trying to override the control matrix. Amazing."

Guillermo's metallic arm suddenly pulled the plasma rifle from his hand and threw it to the floor, the pain in his back a lightening bolt of pain, as if his spine would collapse at the weight of the arm. Out of the corner of his eye he saw Dervish move, but then he realized that she was being carried away by two soldiers, her limp body a rag doll in their hands.

He fought against the paralysis, straining his muscles as the princess approached him, but his effort was futile, and soon she stood before him, her upturned face incapable of expression that he understood but he was sure that she was gloating.

"I have plans for you yet, Terran," she said. "Your survival was at first an oversight, but you have become the best piece on the game board. I will miss playing with you. My benefactor promised that these nanites could be used to frame you, to get you to injure others, cause you to become a pariah to the security force. It has been fun toying with you."

She flicked her hand over the control device and he felt an burning stripe of pain rip through his body as if his very arteries were set afire. He tried to utter a scream, but his lungs seized up, and the convulsive force of every muscle in his body seizing caused him to fall to the floor, his mechanical arm scraping and sparking as it clawed independent of his control.

A mixture of blood and vomit shot from his mouth as sparkling white dots danced in his vision just before he fell deep into a black river of unconsciousness.

CHAPTER 21

Guillermo was awakened by a sharp stinging sensation along the left side of his face, and when he opened his eyes he saw the diminutive princess sans battle armor, her arms and legs clothed in a thick grey garment that seemed puzzlingly utilitarian for a royal. He tried to lift his head but something slithered across his face and pressed against his skin, covering his mouth and squeezing him against the hard slab upon which he was fastened. More cord-like strands tightened as well until he could not breathe, his lungs burning for air, until he heard the princess hiss and the restraints began to loosen slowly, but not enough for him to move.

"Are you familiar with what your species call the strangler vine?" came her voice, somewhat disembodied since he could only see the jagged black ceiling above the table. "It is one of my pets. Something I have been raising for years."

He did not speak, the iron hard vine still covering his mouth.

"It obeys rudimentary commands," she said, her insectoid face now visible above him. "I tell it to grasp or to release prey. It used to thrive in a jungle near New Titan, that now abandoned city your kind founded when they conquered us. Your species poisoned it with your desire to remove the organic from our water supply, an organic that the strangler vine needed to survive, that we needed to survive. Do you know how difficult it is to keep a strangler vine alive these days?"

She touched the vine over his mouth and it shrank away, allowing him to tighten his lips and grit his teeth.

"I don't give a chert about your horticultural hobbies you —"

The vine slapped back down over his mouth and tightened again, and he bit it, only to taste a foul liquid that burned his tongue.

"I wouldn't advise piercing the skin of the strangler vine, Terran," she said flatly. "It is full of the organic. Quite toxic to your species. And I don't want to lose you just yet."

The vine pulled away and he spat at her, now able to lift his head a bit from the slab, and he noticed that several of the spiny tendrils were strapped tightly across his body. He struggled against it, but found himself completely immobile, barely able to breathe under the crushing weight of the vine.

"I am going to release you soon, Terran," she said, her small hand caressing the iron vines strapped across his chest. "And when I do you will be driven into the twisting maze of tunnels here beneath the palace. There I will hunt you down and kill you. Afterward, I will be dining on your flesh. Terran tastes quite divine, actually."

"I hope you choke on me," Guillermo growled, but his face twisted at the news that she knew the taste of Terran flesh.

Just then her wrist comm flickered to life, projecting the shape of bug hieroglyphs, and she had to raise her forearm perpendicular to the floor to read them. She spun around so as to hide the visual segment of the transmission from Guillermo, and he heard the princess speaking what he recognized as Aldrassan, but his knowledge of the language was limited. He had spent five weeks on Aldrassus when he was a cadet. Part of an exchange program. He fully understood how to pronounce "where is the bathroom", "please no spicy" and

"I'm not interested in buying", but it had been so long ago that he didn't understand much else.

He could, however, read the princess's body language. She was somehow subservient to whomever was on the other side of the wrist comm.

The conversation continued as he watched, and he picked out words such as "hunt" and "mission", and the princess began to shake her head in irritation, but soon she took on the body language of subservience and compliance, an unusual posture for a princess.

The comm winked out, and she spun to face him.

"It appears that my desire to hunt you is contrary to our overall plan," she said. "No matter. I was waiting on the council to arrive. They wanted to see you one last time before I ended your life."

"The Council?" Guillermo said.

"Yes," she chittered. "All but one, of course. He would not follow orders, so we sent him into the Terran enclave with the bomb. Used the nano-controller embedded just beneath his skin to walk him in by remote. It was quite spectacular, really. We needed to eliminate the rest of your kind, cleanse the Five Rims of the vermin. Soon we will launch an armada that the military has been refitting at a station beyond the moon. Our victory over the Ontoccan Hegemony will be glorious."

She snatched a small orb that he had seen before from a nearby metallic table and held it in her hand as the holographic interface winked to life.

The control device for his arm.

"This device has been helpful in painting you as the

monster you refuse to believe you are. I wonder what it would feel like if your arm began to strain against my strangler vine, tried to tear itself free from its bonds with your fragile shoulder as an anchor?"

Guillermo's eyes widened as she raised a holographic bar with her dainty finger that was projected from the orb. His arm began to work independently, his shoulder joint groaning and popping, his teeth grinding as the pain gripped him.

"It won't be long and it will tear itself free of you," she said, leaping up onto the slab with him then with a singularly lithe grace.

She bent down over him, waved the small device in front of his eyes before leaning close to his face. She caressed the vine over his mouth with one small finger and the plant slowly released him, slithering back under the table.

"I will enjoy hunting you, Terran. Listen carefully to my words. This will be the last time anyone will hear your backward language spoken. It is such a limited, foolish form of communication. So inferior to my own. At least we are able to communicate exactly what we mean without all of your confusing metaphors and idioms."

"Well in that case," Guillermo whispered. "I suppose you should read my lips carefully when I speak my next few words."

Before she could respond Guillermo's metal arm broke free of the vine, knocking the device from her hand and shattering it against a nearby wall. He gnashed his teeth at her, raising his head enough to bite down on her lower mandible, the little claw on the end of it piercing his lip. He bit down until he heard a crunch, and she pulled back and fell to the floor, tearing one of the tender finger-like appendages from her face. The vine began to tighten on him then, wrapping around his extended metal arm, but he managed a laugh before it squeezed the air from his lungs, the blood from his severed lip running down his chin as he spat the left mandible onto the floor.

She hissed, pointing at him and crouching as several soldiers filed into the room, their plasma rifles raised. She raced at him, her fist pounding at his face until his cheekbones bled and his eyelids began to swell. Her soldiers stood silent, watching the fray as if mesmerized by it, and soon she backed away and he could faintly hear the sound of her abdomen breathing the thick, humid air, a damp wheezing sound.

He rolled his head to the side, spat a copious amount of blood and saliva, and through squinting eyes grinned at her, a maniacal laugh echoing in the small room.

"Hunt me, you crulling brat," he coughed. "I'll make sure you never forget the Terran people, or at least I'll be so disagreeable I'll make you sick for weeks."

She did not respond, the damage to her mouth preventing her from speaking. With a motion of her hand the vines released him and every soldier in the room trained their rifles on him, her crouching posture and the wagging of her head telling him everything he needed to know. He swung his legs over the edge of the slab and dropped to the floor, swaying a bit, his balance compromised by the raging headache that the princess had given him. The coppery red blood filled his mouth and he spat it out again, knowing full well the sensory overload it caused for the bugs around him. At the princess's command they backed away and made a path that led to the tunnels outside.

He was forced down a smooth hallway, and standing behind a row of soldiers stood the seven remaining council members he had seen in the Queen's audience chamber, their hisses of disapproval clearly audible to him in the eerie silence.

Soon Guillermo entered a room with three exits, a green-skinned soldier posted at each one. He wiped his mouth with one hand and turned to face his captors. Several soldiers filed into the small room before the princess appeared again. She strutted in front of him and one of the soldiers handed her a long thin rifle, and he recognized it right away.

It was one of the rifles he'd used from Junior's weapons stash. Mounted to the barrel was an elongated scope, its lenses glowing with a soft green light.

She motioned to a familiar soldier with a scarred face. He stepped forward to translate for her, the princess's injured mandible still oozing fluorescent blood.

"A helical rail gun," said the general as the princess held the gun before her inspecting its angular lines. "Her majesty says our soldiers will soon be outfitted with these after we work out the details with the supplier. It seems she lost a shipment of them in a fire. The weapon fires through solid dura-steel and each one is equipped with a scope that allows it to see heat signatures through several meters of solid rock."

"Now that's just cheating," he said, indicating the gun. "You sure you don't want to just duke it out right here? These goons can watch me go easy on you."

She leaped into the air and kicked him across the jaw. If not for the soldiers holding him in place he would have fallen to the floor.

"I-i-i will s-shooze the metho-o-d off your demis-s-se," she stammered, spitting glowing blood on him.

She motioned with one hand and they released him, the soldiers by the exits stepping aside. He spit one more blob of his own blood at the princess's feet and stood before the exits, then jogged through the passage to the right, down a darkened corridor, and nearly hit the wall as the passage curved to the right and then down.

He could just see the round yellow light of the doorway behind him when he turned around, and he thought about charging back toward them and taking his chances with the soldiers up close, but he continued on. He felt along the walls, trying to move as briskly as possible, but the further he moved from the first room the darker the tunnel became. Soon he reached an intersection, then another, then another, and he moved straight ahead in hopes of reaching an exit.

After the fourth intersection he stepped off into a void and fell, tumbling to the bottom of a pit that was thankfully only a meter or so deep, and when he stood to his feet he sensed someone else nearby.

A scream rose in his throat as a hand touched his arm.

CHAPTER 22

"Guillermo," chittered a bug voice in the dark. "Do not fear."

"Dervish!" he exclaimed. "How did you...?"

"I was briefly detained, and for that I apologize," she said. "The blast from the plasma rifle cascaded across the armor plate I had stolen and stunned me momentarily. Someone killed the soldiers who carried me away. It was the female again...the Terran. The soldiers were only obstacles for her, as she was clearly targeting me, but I escaped down a ventilation shaft."

"Terran," Guillermo said, his voice even and low. "Are you sure? Do you think someone survived the bombing?"

"This Terran was not interested in talking, Guillermo. She was trying to kill me."

"She?"

A clamoring could be heard down the tunnel, what could only be the princess and her hunting party gearing up for Guillermo's eventual death.

"There is not sufficient time," she said. "The soldiers will be here soon, and I believe we are being hunted."

"I'll do my best to follow you."

He felt her shoulder in the darkness and she grabbed his hand. He held tight as she ran along, and she stopped now and again to warn him when they needed to be wary of more uneven terrain.

But he could also hear the near silent clicking of the hunting party, and after a while he began to long for any form of illumination, the void a cold, foul blanket that robbed him of his independence.

As they neared another intersection, a half meter rod of superheated carbon shot through the wall near his head and embedded itself in the floor. At last he could see in the faint orange glow of the rod, but the idea that he was being targeted through a scope that could see through walls terrified him.

"Stay low," said Dervish. "A small target is a difficult target. It appears that she is above us in another tunnel."

Guillermo did not argue, following Dervish along, and when they rounded another corner and the darkness washed over him again he reached for her hand but instead heard her hiss. His hands instinctively covered his ears as if they could protect him from what was coming next.

Another rod shot through the ceiling directly above them and then pinned his mechanical arm to the floor. The heat from it caused him to scream as the artificial nerve endings relayed the heat of the exuded bar of molten carbon directly to his brain.

"I am sorry, Guillermo," said Dervish. "Forgive me."

She bent down and with one motion separated his punctured arm from the glowing rod, the metal making a screeching whine against the superheated carbon, leaving a gaping hole in his wrist. Guillermo nearly bit his tongue in two as he screamed through clenched teeth.

"You must endure," Dervish said flatly. "We must survive."

She took his hand, helping him up, and they ran along the ever darkening tunnel. After a moment they reached another intersection but this time she led them to the left. Guillermo's thighs began to burn as they jogged up a steep incline.

"Almost there," she said. "I have been in this section before."

He began to see a faint glow ahead as another carbon rod shot by them, its orange light reflecting off of the walls around it as it raced ahead, reaching the end of the tunnel in seconds. Dervish stopped, pressed her hand against a recessed divot in the wall, and a section of it irised in to reveal a white room beyond. On the other side of the room Guillermo saw a great round metal door.

Once inside another rod burst through the wall, burning past Dervish's head and embedding deep in the duracrete. She tucked down and rolled, then shot across the room to activate the security panel with a wave of her hand. The two of them shot through into the lower levels of the palace before the metal door closed behind them.

Dervish led him along a curved, white hall to an open lift just at the other side of another high-domed room. They climbed aboard and she again placed her palm on an activation panel and the doors closed, the lift rocketing higher and higher, heading for the throne room.

"We must warn her majesty of the plot," said Dervish, her head wagging in agitation. "She must not perish."

"The Queen?" Guillermo asked, looking down at his punctured robotic arm. "And how did you get away from the soldiers?"

"I intercepted a message on the air. The princess and the military are colluding together to assassinate the Queen and the Ontoccan delegation, reinstate the monarchy, and declare war on the Ontoccan Hegemony. They see the Hegemony as an impure Terran construct, something built from the root of Terran influence. They plan to eradicate it forever."

"But they are in for a fight," Guillermo said. "The Hegemony owns all the old Terran tech and hoard the knowledge of how to repair it."

"She has gathered defectors of our species who have renounced the Hegemony," she said. "They are helping her repair and modify the warships. As you know, the Ontoccan races were brought in slavery from their home worlds to Ontocca by your ancestors, know nothing of their own culture, and have adopted the culture of their former overlords. The Ontoccans know nothing of their native tongues or customs, their government a benevolent hold-over from the Phaedran Empire. For this, the princess is convinced that they must be defeated in order to restore the balance of the four races of the Five Rim worlds, to restore things to the way they were before the invasion. They plan to eradicate the last trace of Terran influence. She calls it a 'cleansing'."

"Yeah. That's the word she used," said Guillermo, his eyes glancing at the hieroglyphic symbols that indicated their ascent. "If the Hegemony falls then you can bet it won't end there. That cleansing business is just a ruse. When she had me wrapped up in that strangler vine she had a convo with someone on a wrist comm. Sounded important. I think she was afraid of them, not sure. She was speaking Aldrassan the whole time, so I don't know what was said, but she didn't seem to be in charge. The Council is on her side as well. I'm afraid we're the only ally the Queen has at this point, because the security force is controlled by the Council."

"We must not lose hope," she said. "We have to get the Queen to safety, stop this plot somehow. We must bring all of this to the surface, let the public of my world know the truth. They are our only asset."

"We have to try," he said, but his heart told him otherwise.

They rode in silence as the lift slowed to its destination at the highest floor in the palace, and when the doors irised open they readied themselves as the antechamber leading to the Queen's audience room was slowly revealed.

The electro-glaives of seven chamber guards shot toward them.

CHAPTER 23

Blue electricity danced on the razor edges of the electro-glaive blades poised centimeters from Guillermo's nose and all he could do was crack a toothy grin.

"Do you ladies want to give me a break and stand down from attack mode?" he asked. "I'm pretty tired of it, really."

One of the guards answered by allowing a small spark to arc across Guillermo's cheek, causing him to squint and release a short grunt of pain. Dervish was already communicating with them, and in a few moments they lowered their weapons and backing away, forming two columns in front and behind them as one of their number marched away from them, down the ornate hallway.

Dlahuud soon appeared, her mottled red skin a stark contrast to the cotton-white floor length gown she wore. The Aldrassan approached them, and she touched Guillermo's injured metallic arm and grimaced.

"You are to be captured on sight, Officer March," said Dlahuud. "I have been informed that the chief examiner is on his way here as we speak. Perhaps you should wait in the Queen's chamber. She may be able to provide sanctuary and prevent your arrest for a time."

"Sphincter is on his way here?" he asked. "Good. He's the Council's lackey, and he's probably in on the plot against the Queen and the whole Ontoccan Hegemony."

Dlahuud seemed to take this in stride, her face showing no sign of expression.

"Then you must explain this to her personally," she said. "Follow me."

She waved her hand and the guards led them along the hallway to the large doors at the end, just as Guillermo heard his arm emit a tinny squeal. He looked down and noticed that the metal around the puncture wound was reshaping, reforming, popping back into place. The nanites were apparently hard at work.

"Chert," he whispered, his eyebrows raised.

His stomach growled.

The heavy ornate doors to the audience chamber swung open, and inside Guillermo saw the Queen in her golden, shimmering gown. Another Aldrassan dressed in maroon, a Guajiin wearing a fine violet robe, and a Fraaz turned to look at them. The Fraaz reclined on a hover skiff, his fine iridescent fitted vest tailored to accommodate his huge wings.

The Ontoccan delegation, he presumed.

A wide window had been opened to the right, a sweeping oval with smooth edges big enough to fit a hover-car through. The skyline of Royal City was outlined just beyond with the orange light of the setting sun. A sheer golden curtain fluttered in the breeze as the wind entered the room and stirred the buzzing phosphorescent insects near the ceiling.

Guillermo nodded his head curtly at the delegation, then stepped forward to address the Queen. Dervish joined the guards, all of them bowing prostrate before her. Guillermo's body guard had formed up with her squad again, and if he had not spent so much time with her he would not have been able to pick her out among the others.

"Your majesty," Guillermo said loudly, grabbing an ulmfraa fruit from a nearby ornate silver bowl and taking a huge bite. "Your life is in danger. The princess is plotting to kill you and the Ontoccan delegation in order to start a war. She wants to cleanse the Hegemony and reinstate all four separate governing bodies of the Five Rims. I'm pretty sure Aldrassus is in on it, too."

"Excuse me," said the Fraaz, his leathery wings folded around him as he lay on the hover-skiff. "Are you the only Terran who remains? How fascinating."

Guillermo nodded, his face tightening as he chewed the ulmfraa, a line of red juice running down his chin.

"What could possibly threaten us?" asked the Guajiin as he folded his lower set of arms. "I doubt anyone could raise a significant enough force to attack us. And why would they? We hold this fragile peace together, allow you all to live in harmony, keep your own governments."

The Fraaz delegate blew air from his spoon shaped nose.

"All Terran tech is under our care. They cannot repair their tech without our engineers. It is part of the treaty of the Five Rims."

Guillermo cleared his throat, then looked at his metallic arm which had now completely repaired itself.

"Oh, the black market is a booming business, apparently. I've seen it first hand. And we've seen the troops, too. They are being armed and trained under the palace as we speak."

The three delegates looked at one another and the Queen tilted her head toward Guillermo.

"Look," Guillermo pleaded, finishing off the fruit. "I barely escaped with my life. The princess was hunting me just below the palace. She's planning something really big and we are really pressed for time. We have to get you out of here."

The Queen emitted a soft clicking like the measured notes of a clock, stared intently at Dervish for a moment, then moved three steps toward Guillermo.

"My servant corroborates your story, Officer March, and it appears that I have been deceived. This is dire, indeed."

"We have to get you someplace safe, your majesty," said Guillermo. "And I mean crulling now."

The Aldrassan delegate took in a hissing breath.

"Waging war against us is futile," he said, his six fingered hands forming a small pyramid. "We are more than equipped to repel any incursion. That is if you are telling the truth. Perhaps this Terran has grown mad with grief."

Dlahuud moved to the mammoth doors and then ushered the chamber guards into the antechamber outside with a command. Dervish slipped through the doors just as Dlahuud was closing them, and knelt in the floor by the window, her head bowed in reverence. Dlahuud activated the latch on the doors and then sealed them via a security panel built into the oversized engraved silver handle.

"I agree with Guillermo, your majesty," said Dlahuud, arms spread to her sides as she approached the delegates. "We should do something…at least until we discover the truth."

"What she said!" Guillermo shouted. "I was crulling *hunted*! She is going to do the same to you if you don't get the chert out of here! All of you! Don't you have a hover vehicle handy? Out that window there?"

The Guajiin folded both sets of arms and glowered at him.

"I would like to reiterate that our forces are too great, Terran," he said. "I appreciate your concern, but this unsubstantiated claim of yours…"

Just then a black armored fist surrounded by an aura of yellow energy protruded from the Guajiin's chest, spraying his black blood all over the Aldrassan delegate who shielded his eyes with his quivering hands. When the Guajiin sank to his knees then toppled to the floor, Dlahuud stood over him, a wicked grin forming on her blood drenched face.

"I so hate the smell of the Guajiin," she said, her skin flickering and pixellating to reveal a tall Terran woman, her face hard, her jet-black hair tied back in a tight bun. "Their penchant for not bathing is proof of their primitive state."

Guillermo's mouth dropped open, speechless at seeing another Terran. He took one step forward, reaching for her briefly.

He tried to speak, but his mouth wouldn't form words, and he only stammered as his mind reeled that she was at the heart of the conspiracy, that she was the Aldrassan voice on the other side of the princess's transmission.

Before he could move, the Terran's black armored hand, crackling with energy, shook the Guajiin's blood across Guillermo's face. Silently she spun and crushed the head of the Fraaz on his hover-skiff behind her in a motion aided by the thin-weave powered armor she wore. Out of the corner of his eye Dervish moved almost as fast, shooting across the floor toward the Terran, an electro-glaive extending to life, but the Terran turned on Dervish and opened her other armored hand. A booming wave of energy exploding outward, rippling the air around her and knocking Dervish across the room and out the open window as if she were a dry leaf in a summer breeze.

"I really wish the princess would have done what she was told and just kill you," said the Terran. "But now I guess you can be blamed for the death of the Queen, traitor. Now the war will begin as planned, destabilizing these feeble governments of theirs, and we can begin to take back what was ours. I guess you can watch the Hegemony and the Five Rims crumble around you if you survive the day."

Guillermo jumped between the Queen and the Terran female, her flexible black armor ornately detailed with the images of human skulls.

"Run, your majesty!" Guillermo shouted, and he thrust forward with his metallic fist, the blow deflected by what appeared to be a square field of energy that suddenly blurred out the female Terran's features on the other side.

She laughed then, and it was a terrifyingly primal sound.

She reached out her hand and he noticed only a blue flash before he was hurled away. Fighting to stay awake he lay on the floor gasping for breath. He raised his eyes in time to see the Queen's chest exploded by the electric touch of the Terran's energized gauntlet. She did not scream. Did not make a sound.

Guillermo screamed for her, his voice raspy and dry.

He watched helplessly as the Terran tossed a small grey dodecahedron in the air. It floated in mid-air, grew steadily, becoming a medium-sized chrome sphere that reflected not what was in the room, but a place that was black and orange. A place with the warped shapes of other Terrans who turned to look at him, their faces elongated in the spheroid glass of a mirror, all of them wearing the same black armor.

Other Terrans.

Phaedran Terrans.

But they were dead, sent out into space to die in the decrepit world ships that brought them to the Five Rims. How had they survived?

He was no longer alone, but somehow wished that he was if the Phaedran Empire was still intact.

The Terran female turned to face him as the solid thumping sound of someone trying to enter the doors could be heard just outside. She smiled wickedly as she dove toward the sphere, her body elongating around the outside of it, stretching around the side of the sphere to vanish from view.

And then the sphere was gone.

He slowly rolled to his right, his body protesting the punishment of the Terran woman's defensive weapons, but managed to stand, his metal fingers scraping the floor.

He had seen carnage before, but the sight of the Queen and the delegates slain, their lifeless bodies laying before him as if he had done the deed with his robotic fist, and it caused a rage to build in him. He began backing away from it, his head shaking back and forth, his shoulders rising and falling as his breath became erratic.

They would pin this on him. They would say that he killed the Queen, the delegates, and he would be the cause for the war. But that meant that the princess was in league with this Terran, and the princess probably did not know the true identity of her Aldrassan contact.

No one would believe him.

He backed away, stepping closer and closer to the open window, his mind on fire with the face of the Terran woman, the questions spinning in his brain. He looked out over the city, the morning sun just on the horizon, the thin clouds caressing the edges of the skyline, and the heel of his boot bumped the low edge of the window sill.

He waited for the inevitable, staring down at the spires of the palace, their blue lights winking on and off. He did not see Dervish, and wondered if he would have time to mourn her.

With a loud clang the doors to the chamber burst open and in poured the Queen's chamber guards followed by a host of security forces with plasma rifles trained on him. He turned slowly to see the chamber guards hissing and rushing forward, their electro-glaives extending out toward him. He backed away from them, raising his hands in defense.

Just as Sphincter forced his way through the crowd

toward him Guillermo stepped backward through the giant open window and felt the air around him whistle past as he fell.

CHAPTER 24

Guillermo rotated his body, the air rushing past his face, his eyes filling with tears, and he embraced the inevitability of his circumstance, the last decent Terran in existence.

Death seemed a welcome enterprise.

As he fell he passed a familiar shape and a filament line shot toward him, wrapping around his waist and grabbing fast. The line stretched, slowing his descent enough that when he slammed into the palace wall the blow was somewhat diminished.

Somewhat.

He spat a gout of blood from his mouth, watching it fall toward the ground a few thousand meters below. He pushed away from the wall, looking above him, and his face flushed as he noticed that Dervish had attached herself to a protruding exterior light just below the Queen's window and was tethered to him via the sticky cord. Above her, however, a host of bug security forces and chamber guards stood at the wide window staring down at them. The princess crouched in the middle, pointing and gesticulating, and then the chamber guards began running down the wall toward them.

"Do you trust me?" clicked Dervish, one hand holding her side, the other clinging to the L shaped light post.

"Do I have a choice?" coughed Guillermo.

Silently, Dervish retracted the filament line and he began to fall again, the uneven black spires of the palace racing up toward him. In seconds Dervish had caught up with him, wrapping him in a tight embrace before firing the filament gun again at a nearby spire and then they were slowing, the cord stretching and making uncomfortable popping sounds. They swung to a protruding landing pad where several standard palace guards began to race toward them, their batons at the ready.

Guillermo landed legs akimbo as Dervish released him, but she managed to roll to a crouching position and was throwing herself into nearby guards who suffered the force of nature that was her martial art. One of the guards darted past Dervish and struck Guillermo on the back of the neck with a baton. This enraged him, snapping him out of his stuporous daze, and the Terran lashed out with his fist to uppercut the guard, dropping him to the tarmac.

"Hover bike!" shouted Dervish, pointing to a row of them at the other side of the landing pad. A lucky guard caught her along the abdomen just then with his baton and Dervish doubled over for a second, only to shoot one foot out and catch him under the chin.

Guillermo did not waste time, ignoring the cracked

ribs he probably had to sprint across the tarmac and straddle a hover bike. He immediately pulled open a panel with his metal fingers and began probing around inside, adjusting optical wires and biting his lip as if that would help him start the bike faster. He only stopped for a millisecond to flick his eyes toward Dervish who had stunned three more guards before limping toward him holding her side, the other hand holding a baton that had become an extension of her arm.

He turned back to work just as a new pain shot through his right shoulder, the unmistakably hot burning of a plasma bolt. He slumped to the left, his metal hand working feverishly inside the guts of the hover bike, his teeth grinding together in a grimace.

Out of the corner of his eye he could see the familiar blur of Dervish as she diverted her path to sprint across the tarmac toward one of the guards who was looking down the barrel of his rifle for a better shot. She leaped in the air, landing on him with both feet, forcing him into the chitinous floor with such force that the plasma rifle bounced up and into her hand. She turned then, moving ever slower toward him. He managed to jiggle a thread of fiber wire and was rewarded with the loud bang of raw cold fusion power that sent out long bolts of blue lightening from under the bike.

"Your ride is ready, ma'am," Guillermo grunted. "Hop on."

She limped forward, slumping onto the back of the bike as he ignored the pain in his shoulder, taking the plasma rifle from her and slamming it into a socket on the saddle. He thumbed the throttle up to near maximum as a group of seven more guards poured out of an access door that irised open. Plasma bolts shot across behind them as they ramped off the edge of the platform and then plummeted down, down, down. The wind whipped by as Dervish tried to hang on to Guillermo's waist, her legs dangling from the back of the bike as if in free-fall.

He felt his shoulder grind as he tried to pull Dervish aboard, but she was slipping away from him.

"Hang on, Dervish!" he screamed, and somewhere in the back of his mind he knew she couldn't hear him, but he wished she could. He let go of one handlebar and grabbed her wrist with his metal hand, squeezing so tight that he felt her exoskeleton give a little, but she did not hiss or flinch, and his stomach sank he realized that she may have passed out.

The roar of a fusion powered engine ten times as beefy as the bike rumbled behind him. The heat of twin illuma-beams shot out from the nose of a pursuing security force interceptor. Its black wings adjusted and swept back to gain on him, and he could hear the whine of the plasma guns powering up.

He strained his back pulling Dervish closer, swinging her body around onto his lap so that she lay across the saddle, arms and legs dangling. Swiping the control stud with his left boot the empty acids in his stomach rose into his esophagus as he forced the bike into a nose-dive, the ground below him growing closer and closer. Nearing a set of tall industrial buildings, their multi-colored lights strobing to ward off passing aerial traffic, he fish-tailed

around one of the exhaust stacks and dropped another
three hundred meters to the deck below, weaving around
heavy loader trucks and automated fork-lifts.

The security force interceptor did not quibble over the
unfortunate loss of innocent bystanders as it plowed
through the mass of workers and vehicles, its twin plasma
cannons firing away, the leftover obstacles bouncing
violently from its electrified magna-shields.

Guillermo found another narrow alley, and with some
difficulty twisted the handle-bars of the bike to drift
around the corner and smack the back end of the bike
against the wall before he gunned the throttle again. The
rear emitter produced a hushed cough as it failed and
then a rooster tail of sparks shot out behind him as the
back end of the bike dragged the ground.

Guillermo took it in stride, adjusted for the bike's
need to fishtail, and then powered down the engine to
drop to the pavement near the entrance to a yard of
outdoor hydrogen tanks. He hefted Dervish over his
shoulder and then ran rapidly on, the pain in his shoulder
and ribs screaming at him.

Over the high walls of the hydrogen yard the security
force interceptor, its black wings upswept and rotating for
descent, strained its engines as it tried to backpedal away
from the volatile tanks. It hovered several hundred
meters above, the plasma guns searching the rows of
tanks for its prey, daring not to fire into them.

Guillermo walked slowly out into the main path
between the tanks as maintenance crews scurried in
various directions away from him as they evacuated the

area.

He held a plasma rifle trained on one of the large metallic orbs.

"Get any closer and my finger gets a seizure," he shouted. "Back the crull off!"

The interceptor hung in the air for a second as if the pilot considered what to do next, and in response two doors opened on its underbelly and four bug soldiers repelled down dangling filament lines, dropping to the dura-crete below.

Guillermo let out a deep breath, looked to his left where Dervish lay unconscious, and then back at the soldiers who were on the ground in seconds, each of them carrying non-lethal batons yet highly capable of being lethal with them. He scanned around him left and right, and his eyebrows raised a bit when he saw a familiar sign written in bug hieroglyphs.

"Risky," he whispered.

He pointed the plasma rifle at one of the soldiers and fired, the plasma bolt dropping the soldier to the ground, but the residual energy echoing off of his body in the form of small fingers of blue energy that reached out toward one of the tanks. Yellow holographic lights began to flash everywhere but the alarm was silent. He could see from the flashing hieroglyphs that he had three minutes before the entire area was flooded with a fast-hardening foam.

Risky, indeed.

He switched the gun over to rapid fire mode and pointed it at the nearest tank.

"I'm not spitting in the crulling wind here, bugs!"
Guillermo screamed. "Next shot goes right in this tank
here!"

Out of the corner of his eye he could see Dervish
stirring, but then a superheated carbon rod ripped
through his rifle, and spun him to the ground. On top of
the wall the princess, again in her green body armor, was
lining up for another shot.

The soldiers moved in, their batons at the ready, but
the pain in Guillermo's shoulder would not allow him to
think clearly. The shattered plasma rifle lay on the
ground a few meters away. He madly looked around him
for anything he could use for defense, but all he could
manage was to rise shakily to his feet.

The soldiers moved in on him, and he rolled to his left
just as another carbon rod whizzed past his ear.
Guillermo's metal arm pounded a soldier, then pulled a
holstered plasma pistol from the dazed bug, but one of the
soldiers was on him, striking at his knee with the baton.
The pain wracked him, and in the fury of it he pulled the
trigger on the plasma pistol, and a gout of blue flame
blasted toward the hovering interceptor. The energy
rolled down the magna-shield like glowing rain drops, the
shield visible only near the plasma, until it dripped off
onto a nearby tank.

He heard a deafening cough as the tank erupted in a
gout of flame that vaporized the metal surrounding it and
he staggered toward Dervish who somehow grabbed his
arm. The two of them, together with the strength of one
person yet severely weakened by their injuries, fell into

an open hatch and tumbled into a vile river of filthy sewage several meters below.

The fall was aided by the force of the blast as they splashed into the stinking river in which Guillermo now fought to stay afloat. He struck his head on an overhead protrusion that jutted down into the pipe as they were pulled along the current and then he finally gave himself to the darkness.

CHAPTER 25

The marshes.

Guillermo was awakened by the sensation of something slithering by him, something that had come to investigate the wound on his shoulder and then move on. He fought to sit up in the muck, his body covered in the grey slime and filth of the sewer drain, his ribs like shattered glass.

He tried to call out to Dervish but his throat rasped. His tongue had been replaced with sandpaper and the smell of ammonia overwhelmed his eyes and nose. He blinked rapidly and then looked to his left to see a small mound of black moss. Laying across it was the unmistakable hand of Dervish. Seconds passed where he thought that maybe she had been dismembered by the blast, but then the hand began to move and she rose up from the other side of the mound, her face bruised and slashed from the rough journey down the sewer drain.

"Are you damaged?" she asked, her words measured

and even.

He nodded, looking at his dirty wound, a cauterized hole that went deep. He tried to move his arm slightly, painfully, and the growl in his stomach told him that the nanites were hard at work.

He rose, using his mechanical arm for support, but when he moved it he could feel a wrenching in his back, and he absently thought about what that traitor Gunny had said about it ripping out of his body.

"How about you?" he asked, his voice a whisper.

"I am sustained," she said. "I need medical attention, however. We must move immediately. I calculate a probability that they will not assume we are dead."

Guillermo held his wound with his metal hand and stared out into the vine-draped weeping trees and an insect the size of a small bird fluttered by him on a journey elsewhere. He breathed deeply, held it, wincing at the pain in his ribs, and then let it out.

"I guess we're walking," he said. "McFly grew up out here before he moved to the city to get a job with the security force. Maybe we'll find help out there. Somewhere to hide."

"I am with you, Guillermo," said Dervish. "But we are in the open. Let us proceed."

Without another word they began walking, and soon found themselves slogging through an unforgiving marshland that drained the energy from them further, each step a struggle to pull their feet from the muck. They paused when they heard movement in the trees, but mainly it was the fluttering wings of predatory insects that drain the fluids from their prey, and Guillermo was thankful that Dervish could still mask their scent.

After about an hour they emerged in a clearing that spanned a few hundred meters, with only waving grasses between them and a thicket in the distance. As they moved cautiously forward, they noticed that the ground was becoming less damp and muddy, and they were reaching the outskirts of a jungle where McFly had spent his boyhood years.

Soon they neared the thicket, and Guillermo's heart sank when he saw what it was. For as far as he could see in the direction they needed to move, their path was blocked by a dense forest of needle bushes. Their spines harder than most plastics, each barb was filled with a necrotizing poison. Not naturally occurring, the needle bushes were an engineered plant grown around the slave camps that the Phaedran Empire used to harbor prisoners during the occupation.

"What now?" asked Guillermo.

Dervish stood still for a moment, then shoved Guillermo to the ground as a superheated carbon rod shot past them. At the edge of the marsh just their side of the trees stood the princess, small from this distance, but he could see that her long thin rifle was lining up for another shot.

"I hate that crulling thing!" Guillermo shouted. "And I'm tired of running."

They dropped to the ground, laying out flat on the itchy grass, and Guillermo raised his metal arm to shield his face.

Near him, half buried in the muck, was the unmistakable yellowed bone of a Terran skull, a familiar carbon rod protruding from the eye socket.

Guillermo grunted, almost standing to his feet, but then plopping back down. They had reached the princess's hunting grounds.

"We are without weapons, Guillermo," said Dervish. "What do you suggest we do?"

He popped up, slapped Dervish on the back with his hand, pointed at the thicket, and said "Chert! What do we have to lose? We crulling run in *there*!"

Another carbon rod whizzed by them, the signature vibrato of the temperature of the carbon superheating the air around it, and he ran into the thicket, his metal arm shielding his face from the spines. This did not stop the spines from scratching at the rest of his body however, and he could hear Dervish hiss as she plowed through behind him, following in his wake as the bushes tried to close in behind him. She was tough, but soon she grabbed him around the waist with one quivering arm as one of the carbon rods lodged itself in her leg.

He reached back through the thicket and pulled her behind him.

Just as Guillermo thought he would die from the fiery needles that covered the front of his body, his shin smacked something smooth and hard, something buried in the ground, and he toppled over, tumbling into a clearing where several crumbling black walls lay embedded in the marshy ground, a remnant of a Terran structure from long ago. A crowd of bugs, all of them young with various profane etchings carved into their reddish carapaces were suddenly pointing long, slender projectile rifles at the intruders.

It was the Iron Brood.

Guillermo raised his arms, his skin full of the tiny needles, the poison producing little black dots on his flesh. He could only grimace, the pain covering every inch of his stomach and legs, and he looked behind him to see an unconscious Dervish.

Before he could speak, a hot carbon rod buried itself in the chest of one of the bugs and they all shrank back and hissed in unison. In seconds they had fanned out, taking cover behind the cracked and crumbling walls, their guns trained on the thicket where the shot had originated. Guillermo attempted to stand but could only crawl, the needles digging into his flesh as he dragged Dervish behind him. He managed to rise to his knees, and he could swear that some of them had found their way to the cartilage in his joints, but realizing that this was the poison stiffening his movement. He rolled over on his back just as one of the bugs grabbed him by the shirt collar and began dragging him behind one of the broken walls.

It was Gunny's son Junior.

Junior tumbled out into the clearing again and grabbed Dervish, hoisting her up over his shoulder and then laying her beside Guillermo before another carbon rod shot out of the thicket and penetrated one of the crumbling walls behind them.

"Your dad's a crulling v'oshtu," Guillermo groaned,

trying to sit up. "Nearly got me killed by The Skeev."

"Skeev going to kill you anyway," said Junior. "Father only did what he had to for survival of business."

Guillermo's face would have registered surprise at the fact that Junior could indeed speak Terran, the sneaky little bug, but the spines prevented him from doing so.

Mostly the thought of Gunny's betrayal made him freshly angry.

"Your business?" Guillermo grunted. "The princess is going to war with the Ontoccan Hegemony. There won't be any business once the tech is cut off. She wants to cleanse the Five Rims of any trace of Terran influence."

Junior looked at him, his face an unreadable mask.

"We go below," he said. "Talk there."

Junior looked at two of his gang members and they grabbed Guillermo by the arms and began to drag him away, his legs now throbbing due to the hundreds of barbs embedded in his skin. They did the same for Dervish, and within moments they were being carried through a door that opened in one of the ruins, then through a deep tunnel alongside scurrying bugs who carried long projectile rifles.

When they reached their destination they were in a vast underground room flanked by several bugs who looked at them with those blank bug faces, none of them exhibiting the sign language he was used to deciphering. No weird scents and no communication occurred. One of the bugs stepped forward with a medical device that removed the spines through a process of negative gravity. The pain was much worse now. Guillermo tried not to scream but couldn't help it when they reached his more sensitive areas, and then he was given a subcutaneous injection that finally dulled the pain a bit, counteracting the poison. The nanites would have to do the rest, which due to the sudden hunger pangs he knew they were hard at work.

Junior reappeared after they had helped him to stand, and then they were working on Dervish.

"You safe," he said. "I free of life debt."

"Thanks, Junior," Guillermo managed. "But there's one thing you are forgetting."

"I calculate no more help for you."

"The princess is going to war with Ontocca. Going to cut off your business when she cleanses all things Terran," Guillermo said, a wry smile forming across his lips. "And I know where her ships are."

CHAPTER 26

Guillermo's eyes, half-lidded and swollen from the poison, scanned the underground hangar where the Iron Brood kept all of its small arms attack craft. Most of them had been cannibalized from old Terran tech, but there were several fancy modifications visible along the dorsal fins and repulser emitters beneath the wings.

Junior had been busy.

So had his fellow Brood members.

Junior stood with Guillermo just outside a makeshift

infirmary where Dervish lay on a slab, her bodily fluids being replentished using various tubes and some little known herbal remedies.

"Princess not find us," said Junior. "Run weapons market down here since before she born. Father start. Big secret. Only Iron Brood know. We build ships, weapons, you name it. She hunt above us all day, all time. She not ever find us."

"I hope not," Guillermo said. "What about Dervish? How is she?"

"Your friend in trouble," said Junior flatly. "She may not survive."

"She has to," Guillermo replied, touching the bandage where the plasma bolt had pierced his shoulder. "She witnessed something, and she's the only one who can clear me with the Ontoccans...if they'll listen."

"Tell me of ships," Junior said. "We raid."

"I will," Guillermo said. "But I want some guarantees. None of this 'betray the guy you worked with for years' chert. My conditions are three-fold…"

Just then one of the Iron Brood approached the two of them, his body twitching in agitation. A silent command was given, and three long skinny rifles were pointed at Guillermo's head.

"He say you kill Queen, Ontocca delegates," clicked Junior. "It all over news feed. Say you start war with Ontocca, that you work for them, want to see Terran way established again. Big money I turn you over."

Guillermo raised his hands in defense, his shoulder only sore now from the wound.

"I can explain that," he said, his eyes wide. "Like I said, the only witness to the truth is lying on that slab in there. We have to wake her up."

"Why should we? News say you bomb your own kind. They hunt you and offer big chids we turn you in. Chids always more important than loyalty."

Guillermo could feel the cold gun barrels pressing into his back.

"You walk," Junior said. "We put you in holding room until we make contact with Brood member in city. Come."

Guillermo spun on them, his metal hand grabbing the barrel of one of the guns behind him and with a twist it was bent.

"Let me save Dervish!" he screamed, tossing the rifle down the hallway. "I swear a Terran did all this! Probably Phaedran! Just let me help Dervish live! You owe me for saving your life, you crulling bug!"

From the slab in the infirmary came a hiss, and they all turned to see Dervish turn and spit a fluid from her mouth, a wheezing cough echoing in the small room.

"I owe her several life debts," Guillermo said. "I have to repay her at least, and then you can do with me what you will. Extract some of the nanites from my blood and let them heal her. They can remove the poison from her blood."

All of them stood silent for a moment, and then without a word they were forcing him at gunpoint into the infirmary room where a shorter than normal bug felt along Guillermo's mechanical arm and attached what looked like a bracelet with a fist-sized screen attached. He tapped away on some holographic displays and Guillermo could see an enhanced image of the microscopic machines that had saved his life so many times in the past few days. The tech removed the bracelet and placed it on Dervish's seemingly lifeless wrist. As soon as this was done they began pushing him out of the room again.

He fought them, screamed at them to let him stay to make sure she lived, and after a few of them faced the wrath of his metal fist they relented and he stayed. He understood from their body language that they pitied him, the last of his kind…or that they would get their money anyway.

He sat on a nearby stool and all the weight of his bulk sank into it, his arms hanging between his knees, his head bending forward. She was saving his life again even though she was unconscious, and he had to make sure she would be able to confess to these pirates the truth about the death of their Queen.

After a few moments she began to stir. Her mandibles clicked and her mouth membrane softly hissed. He held her small hand in his, his face stern, his lips drawn. He could smell the sweet scent of pheromones in the air, and she raised one quivering finger to point at him before dropping her hand to the slab. She fell asleep then, her breathing no longer a wheeze but a soft slow pulse of air that rose and fell with the motion of her abdomen.

"Where is fleet," Junior said, his gaze falling hotly on Guillermo. "You take us there, and we seek out this

Terran who kill our Queen and start this war."

"Sure thing, Junior. Ever make a run to the moon?"

CHAPTER 27

Guillermo followed Junior to another hangar bay where he saw rows and rows of lightly armored interceptors, heavily modified and cannibalized from various other ships and fighters. Iron Brood bugs were loading up, several of them outfitting the small craft with energy cells and grappling lines that would be used to attach the small ships to larger vessels. Bugs wearing heavy hodgepodge armor and carrying long projectile rifles were boarding trap doors on the back of the interceptors, but only four Iron Brood per ship were able to stow aboard.

Guillermo put a hand on Junior's shoulder and the bug spun around as if ready for a fight.

"Hold on, kid," said Guillermo. "How do you expect to take down an armada with just a few interceptors?"

"Only take one," he said, his body language calming. "The rest we threaten. Salvage big payload."

Guillermo only nodded, his mind burning with the idea that they were all probably going to be killed. He was not confident with Junior's haphazard plan.

Trying not to protest, he was guided to an interceptor where he boarded with three armored Iron Brood bugs who looked at him from behind mirrored face shields, their body language was unreadable. They nodded at him, a common gesture they learned from interacting with Terrans, their demeanor blankly stoic.

After some air traffic control consisting of one bug doing a bizarre dance in the middle of the tarmac with a glowing rod, a fast sequence of hieroglyphs on the pilot's dashboard gave the order to leave the hangar bay and they powered up and raced down a tunnel. The small fleet of craft ejected from a hidden door that irised open along the face of a cliff, banked hard along a canyon, and then splashed through several waterfalls which masked their movements. Each cluster of three ships broke off when they were at a varied distance from the mass, burning a vapor trail of superheated plasma that launched them into orbit in a matter of seconds.

Guillermo's metallic hand gripped a loop of cable on the wall of the hold and strained against the sickening crunch of gravity. They soon felt the weightlessness of space before the gravity generators kicked in and caused him to sit hard on the bench with the other armored bugs. He smiled at them, and one of them actually flicked a finger his way before returning to his impersonation of a statue.

"Guillermo," came the voice of Junior over the comm. "We approach moon now, but military craft on intercept course. We powering down to not be seen. You trust."

"Sure, buddy," Guillermo chuckled sarcastically. "Got it. You're in charge."

Guillermo's stomach reacted to Junior's words much in the same manner as it did when he walked across Death Adder's landing pad outside his lair all those days ago, but then he thought that maybe his nanites needed a meal.

No, it was nerves.

The lights going off in the cabin didn't help the situation, and he let out a sigh, then flexed his metal hand a few times listening to the servos whir.

And then there was a crash, something slamming against the hull outside. Then they were spinning, the proximity alarm an annoying yet fearful sound like the squawk of a massive predatory bird. He reached for something, anything to right himself, to prevent colliding with the inside of the cabin, and grabbed the ankle of one of the Iron Brood who hissed and kicked at him in frustration.

His other hand managed to grapple with the interior hull and he found a solid metal bar to grasp which slowed his spin, but the alarm was squawking and holographic hieroglyphs were flickering and strobing. He pulled himself along in the black, his eyes focused on the cockpit window ahead where the star field swirled and danced around the heavily cratered moon in the distance.

The pilot's head lolled around limply.

Slowly, impossibly, he pulled himself forward, his metal arm the anchor by which he pushed himself into the cockpit. His fumbling fingers disconnected the restraints, pulling them away from the pilot as little globules of florescent fluid shot out of the pilot's neck just as the gravity generators failed. The body bounced out and down as Guillermo forced himself into the seat and noticed that a force field had closed an atmospheric breach ahead of him, a small crack in the plasteel view-screen. He slammed his fist on the alarm system override, shutting off that annoying squawk before his eyes began to scan the control panel for any tell-tale signs as to what the crull was going on.

Engine two offline.

Exhaust line ruptured.

Weapons systems inoperable.

Atmosphere compromised.

"Basically crulled," Guillermo mumbled to himself.

He felt a hand on his shoulder, and craned his neck to see the remaining three Iron Brood looking dead at him.

"Hang on, boys," Guillermo said, pumping a manual control node. "This next bit will stomp your gut so hard your mom will feel it."

Please don't hit us again.

He slammed the throttle open and fired the igniters now that he had vented the plasma into space, hoping that the engine would fire up.

He waited.

A blue gout of plasma shot past the viewfinder.

A deafening boom.

Guillermo felt the force of gravity crush him into his seat as the Iron Brood bugs hung on to whatever they could grasp. The engines, fed by an overdrive of high octane plasma blasted them forward toward the moon as the white orb became larger and larger in the viewfinder. He pulled hard on the stick, the overfed engines redlining. Soon he saw the waiting Iron Brood squadron, ordered to hide in the dark shadow of the moon but instead engaged in battle with a military cadre of military interceptors, firing deadly plasma blasts and doing the dogfighting dance of war.

"Guillermo!" came the clattering voice of Junior over the comm. "We engaged. Knew we were here. Some of us going through with plan. Lead us in. Others protect attack."

Guillermo did not respond, letting his actions be his answer. He pushed the engines, ignoring the warning lights and alarms which sounded again, and felt the hand of a lone Iron Brood on his shoulder tighten as he blasted past the dogfighters, weaving in and out of their plasma blasts. He heard the ding of near misses as he emerged on the other side, racing past the seven waiting Iron Brood ships that followed him as he exploded toward one of the Dreadnaughts.

The armada of Dreadnaughts sat motionless in space, a field of warships each the size of a metropolis, and according to Guillermo's flickering scanner their weapons were not powering up.

"Arrogant v'oshtu," Guillermo muttered.

A spray of plasma bolts lit up the black of space with blue electricity as the Iron Brood converged on their single target, the outermost Dreadnaught. Guillermo's little ship rocked with glancing blows as he sped forward, and when engine number two failed again he compensated with the stick, hoping that the vacuum of space would prevent the engine from igniting the power core. His Iron Brood passengers were already on the move, manning the grappling gun as they approached. He blinked when they fired it, a gut reaction to the clank of the explosive round used to do so, and he watched as the cable penetrated the outer hull of the Dreadnaught, pulling them hastily forward to land on the outer hull with a hollow clang heard within their ship.

A docking tube locked on, and after a quick placement of a shape charge and a deafening boom, leaving a permanent ringing in his ears, Guillermo and crew entered the hold of the ship. He now understood why they all carried projectile weapons.

They had emerged in main engineering, and the crews of military caste were already swarming on them, but the projectile bullets ricocheted harmlessly off of metal walls and engine housings but not so harmlessly through the soft exoskeletons of the engineering crew. Guillermo discovered that the Iron Brood were exceptionally skilled in the art of the redirected bullet.

Soon more holes formed in the hull and the highly adept pirates commandeered the engine room, locked down the access bulkheads, shut down the power supply to the bridge, then re-routed control of the ship to the holographic control panels at the engineering station. This process required many viral overrides and spike programs that had the same effect on the ship's systems as the projectile weapons had on the engineering crew.

They were highly efficient, Junior's plans executed carefully and methodically.

"That part easy," Junior said, slapping Guillermo on the back once he was through his own hull breached door. "Now we jump this ship to asteroid belt, strip down for supplies."

"What about the other ships?" Guillermo said, listening to a steady thump of metal on metal as the crew on the other side of the bulkhead began to attempt to save their ship. "And the crew of this ship. I don't think they'll just sit around and let you jump away. Not only that, what about the fact that they will still go to war with Ontocca. No more business for you, my friend."

Junior stood quietly, his crew silently manning the engineering stations, several of them spinning up the stardrive to begin the sequence for a stable wormhole using negative gravity generators and many other delicate and complicated energy sources.

Bang…Bang…Bang…

"The princess is behind this, Junior. You're really going to settle for this one ship and let all those others start a war that will not only ruin your livelihood but also wreck your world?"

Bang…Bang…Bang…

Junior walked slowly over to the engineering control station and began the dance of command, his body accentuating a pheromonal emission that did not seem to be pleasant news for his crew, who wagged their heads in disapproval.

"We make the hard part harder, Guillermo," he said.

"New plan. You see. It all work out. We get paid anyway."

CHAPTER 28

The six remaining Iron Brood interceptors detached from the hull of the Dreadnaught and blasted away, soon joining the few interceptors still dogfighting the military fighters. The Iron Brood began to cluster together, forming a tight diamond formation and linking their force field emitters to create an angled and direct defense as they blasted through the line, the military ships converging on on their position in a concerted effort.

Junior's heavily modified plasma engines were a bit faster than the military fighters, but since the force field emitters were rotated behind them to stave off enemy fire, the military fighters began to drain the power cells of the pirate vessels.

"Great plan," Guillermo said as another plasma blast rocked his ship. "I guess we just run?"

"Patience," Junior said coldly. "Traitors to Queen meet justice and we get rich. Everybody win."

Guillermo watched the scanner as the Dreadnaught they had commandeered and then evacuated began to adjust its course, veering off into the cluster of Dreadnaughts, its energy signature at a maximum reading. The hacked enemy comm band began to fire off alarmed hieroglyphs, ordering the cadre of military craft to return to the fleet. Something was terribly wrong.

"What did you do, Junior?" Guillermo asked, but the Junior and his crew sat quietly, the pilots feverishly increasing power to the shields.

Guillermo watched the holographic display helplessly as the rogue Dreadnaught reached the center of the formation of starships and detonated, a red-line of energy registering on the scanner, its fusion reactor overloading, and in seconds they felt the shockwave buffet their ship.

"What the chert did you do, Junior!?" Guillermo screamed, straining forward as two bugs tried to subdue him. "Those soldiers were only following orders. They could have been reasoned with! Bargained with! Why?"

But the pirate was without an answer as he typed in an order to his remaining ships to scour the wreckage for parts and equipment. When they arrived at the blast site, some of the Dreadnaughts had jumped away, but others were not so lucky. Twisted hulks spun and wobbled in space, a graveyard of spare parts and retrofitted hardware. Guillermo stood silent as the pirates picked the carcasses of the military ships for parts and supplies, sometimes stopping to celebrate when they found a particularly valuable piece.

Guillermo was only able to sit in silence, his stomach churning.

The salvage operation continued for some time, Guillermo's heart swelling with hatred for what these criminals had done, but unable to do anything, say anything, knowing that his only option was to call in the favor to leave when he had the chance and hope that this scoundrel would honor it, hope that Dervish would be able to join him.

Even though his soul felt tainted to be a helpless part of this operation, he knew that they were only the product of what his race had wrought upon their society.

Guillermo realized the terrible notion that these recent events were set in motion by a Terran, the black armored female who had murdered his only government supporter before jumping away through a chrome orb, a wormhole leading to somewhere unknown. He knew that she was behind the bombing that had made him a lone terminarch, and he swore that he would find her and bring her to justice.

But these pirates. They were going to profit from arming both sides in the war, and he couldn't be a part of that. Their behavior disgusted him.

"I take you home now," said Junior, slapping him on the shoulder as if nothing was wrong.

Guillermo's eyes, filling with the tears that the pirates would never shed, became reddened with rage.

"I don't have a home to go back to," he spat. "Just take me back to see Dervish. Then I'll figure out what you...finally...owe me."

Junior, amazingly, made good on his word, pirate or not. Guillermo assumed Junior was too focused on making money to care. They would cannibalize and repair the parts and weaponry that they had recovered and then sell it to both sides of this impending war.

A few hours later Guillermo appeared at the door to the makeshift infirmary and found Dervish sitting up on the slab staring at her hand. She moved her fingers delicately in a fluid motion.

"I thank you for the chance to live again," she said absently. "I suppose I am to be free of my debt to you in the afterlife, then?"

Guillermo approached her, placing his metal hand gently on her arm.

"Dervish," he said. "I release you of your debt to me. Live a long life. Where I am going you can't follow. I could not live with the guilt if I got you killed."

She turned to face him, her large compound eyes reflecting millions of tiny images of his face.

"You cannot command this," she said. "Only the Queen can break my commitment to you, and she is no more. Her daughter is a traitor and the hand of a greater evil. We must avenge her majesty. We must find this Terran female and thwart her plans. War may be inevitable, as tensions have been brewing for some time, but we must do what we can to end it."

Guillermo did not respond, but leaned forward and tenderly kissed her between her eyes and then left the room. She did not follow.

He asked for a star-drive capable ship and Junior granted it begrudgingly, but stated that he was pleased to be finally free of his life debt. It was a medium size cargo ship, a "fixer-upper" to use an ancient Terran term. Guillermo agreed to take it because it had star-drive and would not draw attention due to its poor condition.

It really was a "fixer upper".

Guillermo didn't know where to start. He had the entire Five Rims to search for this Terran, to find out what her plans were, to discover what had happened to the remnants of the Phaedran Empire. He also had to distance himself from the inevitable war that was now brewing between the Ontoccan Hegemony and the bug world. The news feeds had already begun spewing the propaganda that would raise the ire of the bugs, get them to support the war, send their young off to die for the princess and her "cleansing". The Ontoccans were blamed for the bombing, the murder of the Queen, the attack on the fleet that the princess claimed was constructed for their "defense". Now they were incensed, drowning the minds of the bug home world in the propaganda of nationalism, of restoring their rightful culture stolen from them by the Terrans.

After watching the news feed for hours, growing numb to the constant vitriol and horror of pre-war cheering, Guillermo sat in the pilot seat of the freighter, a ship he chose to name "Terminarch". He moved his hand over the old style motion activated studs, going through his pre-flight checks, having to bang on the console now and again to get the connections to fire, when he smelled the faint aroma of a pheromonal cue and turned to see Dervish standing behind him.

"So that's it, is it?" he asked. "Come to join me for certain death and a possible prison term? Probably death."

"Certainly," she said, her voice flat and toneless. "And

if we are caught I can turn you in for the reward. Or I suppose I could kill you and seek forgiveness from the princess with a gift of your head on the end of my electro-glaive…once I am able to procure one."

"Sure thing," said Guillermo, a smile trying to form on his lips. "Let's get this death party started."

He fired the engines, they hummed for a few moments, then died surreptitiously.

"I will analyze the problem," Dervish said, and she disappeared from view.

It took them a good hour to find it, a tiny beetle that had chewed through some optical cable. All the while he fell back in to teasing Dervish about her lack of emotion, made at least three comments about her parentage, and questioned the validity of her birth at least once.

She didn't say a word about it.

EPILOGUE

She approached the Mausoleum de Computat, her armor black and ornate with the imprint of their muse, their totem, the grinning Terran skull. She strode confidently through the black-metal arch that led to the center of the Hall of Worship, past the Augment Priests, their flesh-embedded goggles whirring, their surgical tools for fingers clicking. When she finally reached the Circle of Wisdom, far across a narrow black bridge across a chasm of glowing orange magma, the Divine spoke to her, the voice a deep rumble as if rising from the core of the planet that powered it.

"Report."

"Phase one complete, oh Computat. May your wisdom illumine our mind and further the species."

"Very good, my child. Begin Phase Two."

Roger Colby is an English teacher by trade, making the lives of teens in his class difficult yet rewarding even if they cannot see the use for the important skills he is teaching them (for the most part). He is a father of four rambunctious children and is husband to a wonderful, beautiful, understanding wife who gives him space to write about weird places and even weirder happenstances. He has many dogs, cats, chickens, and birds.

It is a noisy house.

Other novels by Roger Colby:

The Transgression Box, 2009
This Broken Earth, 2012
Come Apart, 2014

Parts two and three of the FIVE RIMS
SERIES are now available on Roger's website:
The Terminarch War, 2017
The Shibboleth Code, 2018

If you liked this novel (or if you didn't) write
a review on Amazon. It would be much
appreciated. Thank you for reading!